Born in New Jersey with a deep love of music, literature, sports, and art, Steve Terrebush embarked on his journey into the world. Studying Philosophy and Psychology in college did wonders for preparing him for the real world mentally, but not so much in the job market, shockingly. He has spent time playing in bands, working for a living, as well as reading and writing. He is married to his wonderful wife, Tracy, and still lives in New Jersey.

This book is dedicated to my family and friends.

To my wife, Tracy. Your love and support make all my dreams come true. I love you.

Steve Terrebush

BEYOND THE MIDNIGHT SHADOWS

AUSTIN MACAULEY PUBLISHERS™

LONDON · CAMBRIDGE · NEW YORK · SHARJAH

Ordering Information:
Quantity sales: special discounts are available on quantity purchases by corporations, associations, and others. For details, contact the publisher at the address below.

Publisher's Cataloging-in-Publication data
Terrebush, Steve
Beyond the Midnight Shadows

ISBN 9781645751205 (Paperback)
ISBN 9781645751212 (Hardback)
ISBN 9781645751229 (ePub e-book)

Library of Congress Control Number: 2019921276

www.austinmacauley.com/us

First Published (2020)
Austin Macauley Publishers LLC
40 Wall Street, 28th Floor
New York, NY 10005
USA

mail-usa@austinmacauley.com
+1 (646) 5125767

I would like to thank everyone who has taken the time to read what I have written, I am truly grateful! Thanks to my family and friends for the support and for putting up with me, I know it isn't easy. Thank you to Moe Morales Photography for the great promotional pictures. And to everyone who has helped get this book released, I cannot express enough gratitude.

Table of Contents

Under the Willow Tree

Chapter One

"Hello, how is my girl today?"

Julie jumps up from her reading chair in a fright. A quick first glance around the room reveals nothing. *Not again,* she thinks to herself. She goes to the stairwell and looks upstairs. "Hello? Is someone there?" There is no answer. The deep blackness at the top of the stairs is a cold reminder of the vast emptiness of the house. She ascends the staircase with a flashlight in her left hand, reaching for the hallway light switch on the right.

Click. The light bulb burns out and leaves an orange glow in the dark. When she reaches the top of the stairs, she looks down the hall. She can feel a creepy chill in the air. This is not an unfamiliar feeling. She feels someone grab her arm with a pinch. "Ouch!" she yelps. This recently has started to happen to her more often than she likes to admit. She drops the flashlight, and it rolls around on the floor, casting odd shadows on the walls. She turns around, and there is a smoky image of a man's face in the shadow next to her. She starts to fall backward down the stairs.

Suddenly, she awakens in her chair. The morning sun is already shining in through the windows of the big house. It looks so much different in the daylight. It is a bright and vibrant house. Although everything seems a bit too big in the house, Julie likes it because it makes the empty house seem fuller than it actually is. The sitting room has a beautiful big red sofa with gold trim that she hardly ever sits on anymore. Her reading chair is a big wooden chair made of oak with an off-white cushion on the seat and back. The arms of the chair curve down into little lion heads at the front. The floor has dull wood flooring that desperately needs to be cleaned and polished but is still in very good shape. The big Oriental rug in the middle of the room is red with bright golden tassels on the ends. It has some strange pictures woven into it that Julie has never really figured out. Hanging from the ceiling is a bright crystal chandelier. Even though it is high in the room, it always shines and shimmers in the sunlight, casting beautiful rainbows around the house. The house seems like it is a happier place during the day. Julie is also always happier during the day.

Carlton is a typical small northeastern town. Julie has lived in Carlton for as long as she can remember. The people in the town are very courteous and always help each other out. The town rarely has visitors, but the lack of people only enhances the scenic rows of rolling hills and tall trees that surround it. There are very few houses in the immediate area where she lives. Julie truly loves this town with all of her heart. She has always felt an affinity for the town that she could not explain. Everything is always calm and quiet. There aren't any big cities nearby, or even any large towns, to disrupt the country lifestyle. The feeling is always peaceful and sedated.

Julie has always been a special girl. Her only responsibility is working at the lunch counter in town once a week. Most other days she just spends on whims. She usually takes long walks through the countryside or just sits outside for hours at a time either reading or daydreaming. She loves to sit and daydream by the big willow tree in the back of the house. Everything is always provided for her. The bills are always paid, and everything is always taken care of for her. She lives well and never asks for anything more than she has. Her benefactor provides everything she needs even though she has only met him or her once. She can only vaguely remember a towering figure from when she was younger, that said to her, "As long as you remain here, I will take care of you." This makes Julie's life very comfortable. She never looks too much into it because it has been this way for so long and is all that she knows.

She has always been lighthearted and positive, but Julie does have problems as well. Julie can't always remember the things that she should. She can't remember things that most people do; like her early days in school or any solid memories of her parents. She just can't remember those days no matter how hard she tries. It seems like her life began around her 8th birthday, which was almost 10 years ago. Sometimes she will sit and dream for hours of memories she has never had; like driving in an old convertible with her father while the radio plays a Glen Miller tune or some other big band hit. Sometimes she sits and dreams of looking out a city window at happy people walking in the crowded streets below. The sky was always blue on days like this, that rich deep blue that keeps her thoughts adrift. She loves this feeling. It makes her feel calm and relaxed.

Those free and happy feelings are always in contrast to the nights when it is a different feeling altogether. Nights make her feel uneasy in the giant house, and for as long as she can remember, she has always had trouble sleeping. Her house is big and always seems empty. Though there is furniture in every room, she is the only one who fills it. There is always an eerie feeling throughout the house at night. The lights never seem to reach into the corners and trees outside creep against the windows and block out the moonlight. She often reads at night to keep her mind at ease. This, sometimes, helps her forget about the darkness. More often than not, she falls asleep in the stiff reading chair in the middle of the room. Her dreams that come at night are very different from the daydreams by the tree. These dreams are alarming. They always seem to creep up on her, and she usually awakes in a startle. Lately, she has found herself so tired that even during the day she feels like sleeping.

Chapter Two

Every now and then, she takes a walk to the local market. The market is quite a walk from her house, but she likes the exercise, and she loves the market. All of the pleasant people shopping and talking to each other make her feel like she's a part of something. She always says hello to everyone she sees. There is no reason not to, they all are so nice and friendly. It is a fine day for her trip to the market. The walk is always very pleasant, but today it seems to be even better. She wanders over the flowing hills and through the trees on a path that she has taken a thousand times. Every now and then, she will meet someone on the way and stop and talk a little. Strangely, she never finds any animals out by the path. She always hopes that she will see one, even if it is just a little rabbit or something, but she figures that they are afraid and hide when she walks by.

When she gets to the town market, she always meets Alexander. He is a newspaper boy on the corner of Main Street and East First Street. Whenever he sees her, he runs over to say hello.

"Hello, Julie! How are you today? Would you like to buy a newspaper?"

"Not today, Alexander, I am just here for lunch. Is anything interesting happening in the world today?" She always thinks of him as the 7-year-old boy that she first met a couple of years ago. He always has his light-brown hair disheveled, and his face is always dirty. He is a smart kid that seems to know everyone in town. She always figured he has had most of them as patrons for his newspaper sales.

"Not much, really, the same old news. But did you hear that old Mr. Vinton died yesterday? He was about 70, so I guess it isn't that big of a surprise, huh?"

"Mr. Vinton? That is a shame. He was such a nice man. How is Mrs. Wachowski taking it? They always played checkers and chess together in the park." After exchanging a few more comments, she continues on her journey. There is really only one place that she wants to visit today. She really wants to go to the lunch counter. Julie loves to go to Mrs. Anderson's lunch counter. She has such great choices, and her friends are usually there as well. Fruits and vegetables, lunchmeats, and chicken, anything that you could ever want, she has at the counter. Julie wants to get there before it closes today.

This is a fine day at the market, Julie confirms to herself while nodding her approval. The fruits all look delicious, and the streets are crowded with smiling faces. She continues to say hello to everyone she meets in a ritualistic manner until she spies Jack out of the corner of her eye. She turns to look, but he is gone.

She misses Jack's company. They were best friends. He used to come and visit her at her house almost every night. About a year ago, he just stopped coming. She had feared for his safety and went to the police. They had never found anything; they even said that they had no record of Jack working or living in the town. Julie couldn't find out any more information, so, after a while, she never really pondered it further. She is sure that he will be coming back soon anyway. Since then, there are rare occasions like this one when she thinks she sees him in the crowds of town. She always spends the rest of the day thinking about him.

Jack was a big man; he was at least a foot taller than Julie. His blond hair hung in his face when he would look down at her in her chair. He would always flash his bright green eyes when he laughed. His eyes always captivated her. They had a sort of glow about them in the darkness, kind of like a cat's eye does. He had a quiet, calming laugh; one that seemed soothing yet almost stifled, as if to keep it quiet because he was frightened of something. He was always smiling. In fact, she had never seen him without a smile on his face. She would try, sometimes, to imagine him being sad, but she was never successful. He would always burst through with a smile, even in her mind.

They would read books and tell stories to each other almost every night. His life seemed so grand in comparison to hers. His stories would always include fantastic people and places that she did not know. She loved his stories because they made her happy. When he was around, she never thought of anything else. Her thoughts were just of his emerald eyes and ever-present smile. She always loved the way that he tried to protect her from whatever she was afraid of. He would always be there to comfort her. Still, sometimes in the market crowds, she catches a glimpse of him, but he would never be there. It is always her mind playing tricks on her. Knowing not to think too much about it, she just continues on her way.

When she arrives at Mrs. Anderson's, she gets an instant smile on her face. This is where she always finds her friends Mary and Greta. Mary is a chubby woman with dark brown hair. She is about 35 years old and always talks about her children and her husband. She never brings them to the market, but she always talks about them. She is so proud of them. Julie envies her for having a close family. Mary often starts conversations with "That reminds me of when my kids did this" or "My husband did that." Julie finds it comforting to hear her stories since she didn't see her family at all. So, in turn, for a short while, she could be part of Mary's family at least.

Now, Greta is another story. She is a very beautiful woman with black hair and red highlights. She has very deep blue eyes. The kind of eyes you can see yourself in, they are so clear and bright. Her eyes are always moving and studying everything around her. She is also much taller than Julie. Julie often wonders why Greta isn't a model or something very glamorous since she is so beautiful. Greta always seems sad or scared about something. She never really says too much but always smiles at Julie with a devilish smile and has nicknamed her Jules. Julie likes that name. It is good to have a nickname. She has never had one before, and it makes her feel special.

Greta says things like, "Hey, Jules, did you hear that someone died from eating parasites in red meat? I will never eat that again. I'm gonna be a vegetarian! There aren't any parasites in vegetables, are there?"

Julie always finds it funny how Greta kind of overreacts about stuff like that. But she always nods her head and says something comforting like, "Really, that's horrible! I don't think there are any parasites in vegetables. Being a vegetarian is a good idea, Greta!" Then Greta smiles her approval and turns her attention elsewhere, leaving Julie's focal point to return to Mary with a giggle.

After Lunch, Julie picks up some fruit to take home. Mr. Joseph, the clerk at the fruit stand, is a very concerned man. He always tries to look out for her and puts a little something extra in her bags for her when no one is looking. He is very nice to Julie and always insists that someone accompany her home since it is such a long walk. That way they can use one of the carts to carry her bags, and she doesn't have to carry them the entire trip. Mr. Joseph never lets her carry her bags home by herself no matter how much Julie claims she is fine doing it by herself. He usually sends Joanna with her, and Julie really dislikes Joanna. Joanna is never happy about the task either. She never talks or even smiles on the whole way to Julie's house. She thinks that Joanna doesn't like her because she has to walk out of her way to take Julie home. Her eyes are black as coal and have always intrigued Julie. How can someone have such perfectly round black eyes? They seem so empty.

Joanna is about Julie's height. She has a thick New York accent and long dark black hair that is pinned up in a bun. Her nametag is always pinned wrongly on her shirt and clicks against the buttons of her shirt pocket while she walks. She wears the same button-down shirt every time Julie sees her. Sometimes Julie tries to count the clicks on the way home, but she always loses count. She starts to giggle to herself realizing how silly it is to count the clicks in the first place, only to have Joanna give her a quick disapproving glare.

Once at home, she can't help but think of Jack. She misses him very much. She remembers all of the time they spent together. She was happier then. Not that she is sad now, but she does feel lonelier now that he has been gone. Jack's crystal-like brown eyes would sparkle when he would bring her gifts. There was the pillow he brought her for her reading chair, but she lost it soon after. It seems that she loses a lot of the things that she gets from time to time. And not just the things from Jack, but also other things that she gets from town also. For example, there was this one bracelet that was given to her by a stranger in the market a long time ago. It was very beautiful. It was shiny silver with a red ruby in the center. Strangely, there was an odd engraving on the bottom that read the name: Reed, Martha. She never understood the bracelet's meaning, but she figured that Martha was the person who owned the bracelet before. Even more peculiar was that she had never seen the man who gave it to her, before or after. He was a short man with dark-black hair. His glasses were too big for his face, but they did give him character. He didn't say anything to her when he put it on her. He just smiled and then left. A few weeks later, it was gone when she woke up one morning. She remembers looking everywhere for it and crying to Jack because she had lost it.

"See if she can feel this?"

She turns around. Nothing. As she scans the room, she starts to yawn. She must be tired, she concludes. It is already starting to get dark again anyway. She turns on the light by the reading chair. Tonight, she really doesn't feel like reading though. All she can think about is Jack. While massaging her left arm, she scans the room. Since it is a nice evening, she decides to go outside and look at the stars. She opens the door and leaves it half open so that some of the hallway light shines outside on the dark field. Once outside, she sits down in the tall grass and looks around the field. The light from the hallway is shining directly on her, so she feels safe and calm. Staring up at the sky, she finds it odd that there is not a star in the night sky. There is just the faded moon, which hauntingly seems farther away than she ever remembers seeing it. The air is stagnant outside right now, and that just adds to the eeriness of the night. At that moment, she hears someone whisper to her.

"Hey, can you hear me?"

"Hello?" she answers as she looks around the field, looking for the voice.

"Shhh. Talk quietly. Do you know what's happening here?"

"Where are you? I can't see you," she replies. She then hears the door slam behind her with the sound of a faint scuffle. She shuts her eyes with fear. "Hello? Are you OK?" There is no reply. Opening her eyes, she turns to the door to reopen it, but it is already open just the way she left it. Starting to be a little more frightened, she decides to go back inside to relax and read, concluding that it is her mind playing tricks on her again. Just before she steps inside, she takes another look around for the source of the voice. The field is still silent and steady. Julie continues to walk inside. She is very tired tonight; all the walking today has made her exhausted. She should sleep well for a change. Once in her chair, she begins to read *A Doll's House*. She can barely make out the words though. Her vision starts to blur. She rubs her eyes and tries again. As she looks up from the book, she sees someone peeking into her window. It is just two cold eyes glowing in a shadow. She quickly jumps up in a panic. She runs to the window, grabbing a lamp on the way. The lamp is a heavy one; if she hit the intruder with it, she should be able to get away. By the time she gets to the window to look outside, the eyes are gone. Wait a minute? Didn't she grab a lamp on the way here? She wasn't holding anything now. The lamp is still on the table by the sofa. Now she begins to hyperventilate. "What is going on?" she yells at the top of her lungs while gasping for her breath.

"You just don't understand yet," warns the same voice from the field. "Here they come again. You better calm down."

Julie screams and starts to cry. The room starts to spin. She feels someone grab her. "Who is there?" she sobs. The room fades darker. In the distance, she hears laughing, and then a bright light hits her face. She cannot see anything. There are faint shadows of two figures around her. She is so frightened that she can't speak. She feels helpless and dizzy, and then passes out from fear.

Chapter Three

Julie awakens in her bed upstairs. She feels strangely refreshed. Was last night just another nightmare? She looks around, and everything is normal. The sun is very bright today, more so than yesterday. The field is motionless in the background of the window. She gets dressed and heads downstairs. The house is glowing with the sunlight beaming in from the windows. There isn't any evidence of the strange occurrences from the night before. The lamp is on the table and the windows are all closed and the curtains are in their normal positions. Her nerves are still a bit shaky from her dreams.

She doesn't feel like going anywhere today. Maybe she will just sit by the willow tree and daydream or hang around her house and relax. She always looks forward to her daydreams by the tree, and they would be a welcome change since her nightmares have been getting worse at night.

She walks to the front door and opens it. Pondering her dreams, she stands in the doorway as a light breeze crosses her face. She blankly stares at the beautiful scene outside, but Julie is numb to all of this beauty that surrounds her today. Her thoughts revert back to her dream and then, oddly, to Jack. If he would be around, he would know how to console her. He always did. He would look at her with those heavenly blue eyes and say just what she needed to hear.

"Everything is alright, Julie, everything is just fine."

She imagines him holding her head on his chest while they sit on the red sofa together. His smile illuminates the dark room. Looking up at him with her glassy eyes, she asks, "Jack, why did you leave me?"

"I never left. I am always with you," he says as his fingers flow through her long blonde hair. "Whenever you need me, you just need to call for me, and I will be there for you."

Julie opens her eyes and finds she is sitting outside next to the willow tree, by herself. Her face is lined with tears. "Jack? Jack, where are you?" The wind lightly blows through her hair. The warm sun bathes her face. She looks around the area and wipes her tears from her cheeks. As she begins to realize she is alone, her eyes start to well up again. Her tears stream down her face, and she then closes her eyes tightly and shakes her head violently, trying to shut out the world.

She opens her eyes slowly. As the blurry world starts to fade into focus, all she sees is red. She jumps up quickly. "Where am I?" she wonders in a panic. After a moment, she realizes she is on her sofa by her reading chair. There is a plate of fruits cut up on her little table next to the lamp. Looking around, she is confused. "Hello? Jack?" How did she get inside and where did the fruit come from? An unfamiliar feeling of warmth and comfort swallows her. She hasn't felt this since the last night she spent with Jack. She is weak from hunger and quickly devours the fruit.

Afterward, she walks upstairs, looking for evidence of who had helped her inside and gave her the fruit. "Hello?" she calls tentatively. When she reaches the top of the stairs, she notices the hallway is completely empty! There is no furniture around and the rug is missing, exposing the wood flooring! Only the sun's rays, which are cascading through the octagon shaped window at the end of the hallway, fill the void walkway.

Suddenly, a small stuffed bear is sitting in the middle of the sunlight. It is white with a tag on its ear that reads, "Martha." Slowly, the bear starts to turn red. Blood starts to ooze out of the bear's body and gather in a pool around it. Julie quivers and closes her eyes in terror.

"Not now," she mutters.

"Hello. My name is Sam. I am here to help you," a voice from behind her calmly states.

She turns around abruptly and is face to face with a kind looking woman wearing a flower print sundress. Startled, Julie takes a step backwards to get a more complete look at her. Giving a confused smile, she looks the woman over. The woman is wearing dress shoes. The woman is about Julie's height and medium build. Her light-red hair is neatly pulled back in a bun and calls attention to her red lips, which are flashing an accommodating smile. Her glasses are small with thin frames and fit perfectly on her nose. They immediately bring attention to her pale blue-green eyes. This woman looks like an old friend to Julie, which she finds odd because she doesn't think they have ever met before. Sam holds her hand out toward Julie and shakes her hand.

"It is nice to finally meet you. How about we talk in here?" she asks while pointing to the door at the end of the hallway.

Leading the way, she brings Julie into the room at the end of the hallway. As they pass through the sunlight, Julie feels the warmth of the summer day outside. Julie pauses for a moment in the sun and closes her eyes. The warmth feels so good that she lets out a soft sigh. Julie then opens her eyes and looks down the hall for Sam, who is standing at the door looking back at her. Sam opens the door; Julie's hair blows in her eyes from the wind. This is a room that Julie never goes into. She did not even know there was furniture in the room. Julie stops to brush the hair out of her eyes before fully entering the room. The room is very well lit and has a faint scent of incense. On the walls are various pictures of Julie throughout her childhood.

"How did these get here?" she asks Sam while pointing at a photo of her on a swing as a child. "I never even knew this was here."

"How did what get here? Please come have a seat next to me, and let's talk," Sam responds as she sits in a chair at a sewing table. Julie then sits in the tall white chair in the center of the room.

"So, what is your name again?" Sam asks softly.

"Julie, and excuse me, I don't mean to be rude, but how did you get into my house?" she retorts quickly.

"So, this is your house? How long have you lived here, in this house?" Sam inquires with a confused look on her face. "Do you live here alone?"

"I have been here for as long as I can remember. In fact, I don't really remember not living here. I never come in this room though. I usually stay downstairs. Are you a friend of Jack's? He used to come here often, but he hasn't been around in about a year."

She realizes how fast she is talking now and takes a deep breath to calm down. She starts to feel uncomfortable in the hard leather chair and starts to shuffle around, trying to get into a better position. She notices that Sam is drawing and scribbling into a black book now. Julie wonders why Sam has not been giving her straight answers at all. As Julie tries to see what Sam is writing, she continues to rapidly ask questions.

"How did you get to my house? Did you carry me in from next to the tree by yourself?" Julie starts getting excited and starts to panic a little.

"I had Raul help me bring you in here because you were laying on the ground outside in the yard," Sam explains and then retorts, "did you say a tree?"

"Yes, the big willow tree outside. Where is Raul? Did he leave?" Julie calms down and starts to feel faint.

"Are you OK? You look a little weary. Do you need anything?" Julie hears Sam say, but her voice is fading and the room is turning black.

Julie starts to stand up and sluggishly says, "I really haven't been feeling well and would like to lay down for a minute. You can stay for a while if you like."

"Sure, I will stay if you'd like me to," Sam replies in a questioning tone.

As she starts to walk, she feels the room start to spin. Julie falls into the small couch in the corner of the room and shuts her eyes.

Julie feels the wind blowing through her hair. As she opens her eyes, she notices that she is outside by the willow tree again. What a dream, she thinks to herself as she fumbles to her feet. The sun is starting to go down now. The sky has turned bright reddish orange. How long had she been asleep? At least this was a peaceful sleep. She starts to walk toward the house, when she notices the house seems further away than usual. She starts to walk faster toward it. It isn't getting any closer. Julie starts to feel scared. Now she is running at full speed. She cannot feel her feet moving below her anymore, she is numb from exhaustion. Still the house is the same distance away.

The sun finally sets, and the moon faintly offers a faded glow overhead. She stops and looks for the house. She cannot even see it any longer. As she turns around, the willow tree looks like a giant spider creeping closer to her as she stands staring up at it. It seems bigger or, actually, it is more like she is smaller. The tree branches seem to be reaching out toward her with the spaces between the branches looking like eyes staring at her. She had not moved from beneath the tree but had been running for what seemed about 15 minutes. "Is this a dream?" she asks out loud.

In the distance, a light comes on in the house. Julie starts running in the direction of the house again. This time, the run seems productive. Slowly, she draws near to the house. Once she reaches the front door, she stops and takes a few deep breaths. As she opens the door, the doorway transforms into the room upstairs. She finds Sam sitting at the table next to the white chair. She is writing in a faded blue notepad this time. She doesn't seem to notice Julie has come in. She closes the door softly. Just then, Sam looks up,

30

stops writing, and stands up. She starts to walk toward Julie at the door.

"Do you feel better now?" she asks Julie.

"Yes, thank you. Have you been here the whole time? Since you are still here, would you like to sit and read with me?" Julie inquires, still a bit confused as to how she got into the room.

"Sure, afterwards we can talk a little more. What would you like to read?" Sam asks as she places her notebook on the table. Sam walks over and sits on the couch. She looks over at Julie, who is still standing in the doorway.

"I have this book I have been reading lately, it is called *A Doll's House*. I can run downstairs and get it if you would like," Julie asks while reaching for the door handle.

"Isn't this it right here?"

Sam shows her the book on the table and taps her hand on the sofa next to her. Confused, Julie grabs the book and sits next to Sam. Julie is instantly comfortable. She opens the book to the last passage that she read and hands the book to Sam. There is a strange, calm, easy feeling about Sam's voice. It makes Julie think of Jack for a moment. She pictures his face and his bright, clear gray eyes and then quickly sets her focus back to the story that Sam is reading. With her head on Sam's shoulder, she looks up at her. Who is this woman, and why is she so nice to Julie? Why does Julie feel so comfortable around her? Questions like these pass through Julie's thoughts as Sam reads.

Julie feels her eyelids getting heavy and lies down on the sofa with her head on Sam's lap. Julie wonders why she is tired if she had been sleeping all day. Sam pauses and then returns to reading. She gently runs her hand over

Julie's hair. Julie lets go of the questions in her mind and gives way to the comfort of Sam's voice. As Julie fades into a light sleep, she hears Sam's voice fading in the distance, reading the play. Her dreams begin to slowly creep into her mind as the room gets darker.

Chapter Four

"Hello, Mommy!"

"Hello, dear, how was school today? Did you learn anything new? Daddy said he will be home soon and not to worry."

"We learned about Christopher Columbus today! Did you know that he discovered America by mistake? He was really looking for India! Did Daddy say he was gonna come to my school play this Friday?"

"Yes, we will both be there, honey. Have you practiced your lines?"

"I have, I am excited that I get to play the lead role in the play! My friend Billy gets to play the hero. We wrote the play in class; it was so much fun. I can't wait until you see it, you will be so proud."

"Of course we will, baby, we love you and are always so proud of you!"

Julie awakens suddenly! Where did Sam go? Julie is lying on the red sofa in her house downstairs, and the book is on the table next to her, but where did she go?

Someone whispers in the distance, "Is she OK? I wish we could help her."

Then she feels a familiar numbing sensation. This cannot be happening. Why is she hearing these things? Is her house haunted? She gets up to survey the house again but, still, finds nothing. She starts to walk up the stairs but pauses as she starts to feel weak and dizzy. As her vision starts to blur, she notices a dark figure moving in the corner. She feels herself start to pass out. She tries to fight it, but the feeling is overwhelming, and she collapses at the bottom of the stairway.

"Daddy's home!" The little girl starts running toward the front door.

"Hello, my big girl! Come give me a great big hug! I missed you so much today!" The father holds her and carries her into the kitchen, where the mother is standing. He walks over and gives the mother a kiss on the cheek. "Hello, dear!"

"Are you excited about my play, Daddy?"

"Of course I am, that is this Friday, right? Have you been practicing?"

"Yeah, and it is gonna be great!"

"OK, baby, it is time to wash up for dinner." The mother gently nudges her out of the kitchen toward the stairs.

Julie struggles to open her eyes. She can barely make out the outline of three figures standing over her. She tries to reach out to grab them but can barely move. Her arms are immovable, but she cannot discern if she is too weak to lift them or if something, or someone, is holding them down. She hears the rumble of voices but cannot make out what they are saying. She finally surrenders to the need to close her eyes.

"Today is the day for the play, Daddy!"

"I know, dear, we will be there, and you will be great! Do you have your costume ready yet?"

"Mommy is finishing it now. Do you think that there will be a lot of people there? I hope so. This is gonna be the best day ever!"

"Your mother will bring you there early so that you can get ready with your classmates. Then we will be there later before the show starts."

"Honey, your dress is ready!" The little girl runs to get her costume from her mother. The doorbell rings in the background. Father stands up and goes to the front door. The little girl comes running excitedly. There is a towering figure in the doorway shaking the father's hand and smiling widely. The little girl jumps into the man's arms and, in one swift motion, hugs him tightly.

"Hello, Uncle Mack! Are you here to go to my play?"

Julie wakes up, and it is morning again. She sits up on her living room sofa. She feels more refreshed today, but nothing really seems as clear. Rubbing her eyes and stretching violently, she looks around the room. She shakes her head to make sure she is awake. After reflecting on the night before, she decides that today she will go back into town to see Mary and Greta. They must be concerned since she hasn't gone to the market in a few days. As she walks to the market, she feels a bit different. The road beneath her feet feels colder and harder. She feels her feet clicking on the ground, as if she were on a hard surface instead of the soft dirt road. The sun doesn't seem as bright today either. She pauses and looks around the road. The trees are encroaching on the road so close together they almost form a wall along the sides of the road. She stops and stares into the trees, as if almost in a trance. She suddenly recalls a painting that she once saw. It was of a road similar to this one, but it had a creek and a bridge in the middle. She struggles to remember where she saw that painting. After a few moments, she concedes to herself that she cannot remember. She thinks to herself that maybe she is still groggy from the lack of quality sleep she has been getting lately. For the rest of her walk, she is preoccupied with the thought of the painting.

As soon as she gets to the market, she notices that it isn't as busy as it usually is. She walks toward the corner where Alexander usually works, to ask him how everything has been, but his shop is empty. There is no one even at the corner. She stops to try and ascertain what is happening but cannot come up with an explanation. The few people that are walking about the streets are not the happy masses that normally frequent the market. These people are sad and stare at the ground instead of acknowledging everyone else. They all are dressed similarly as well; everyone is wearing drab grayish-white clothes. She walks toward the lunch counter and grabs her food. Julie still can't understand where everybody is. Scanning the room, she notices Greta sitting in the far corner. She briskly walks over to sit next to her.

"Hello, Jules," Greta says with a half-smile. "You haven't been out in a while, have you?"

"No. I haven't been feeling well lately. What is going on around here? It seems so very different," she asks observantly as she studies the large, nearly empty room.

"Really? What seems so different to you?" Greta retorts in an almost snotty tone. She examines Julie with a menacing glare. "What, are you having bad dreams again? So, finally, the world isn't all sunshine and flowers for you." Greta shakes her head and mutters, "Whatever, Jules."

Greta stands up and starts to walk away. Julie awkwardly grabs her arm and holds on tightly. As she does this, two men from the crowd look at each other and begin walking toward them.

Looking terrified, Greta whispers, "Please let me go, they are coming over here."

Suddenly, Julie is reminded of the whispers from the field. She gently lets go of Greta and sluggishly turns her head toward her meal. As Greta walks away, the two men stop, mumble something to each other, and turn away. Disheartened and bewildered by the day's occurrences, Julie sits and stares at her cut up fruit and juice. What is going on here? Why was Greta acting so strange? These questions keep repeating in her mind without answer. A few minutes later, Mary sits down across from her. She is also wearing a drab white shirt. Mary doesn't say a word; she just sits and plays with her soup. It must be some kind of chicken soup because Julie can smell the broth across the table. After about two uncomfortable minutes of silence, Mary looks up at Julie. A small faint smile crosses her lips.

"Hi, Julie. Are you feeling any better today? I heard you the other night. You seemed quite frightened. Raul said he would check on you to see if you were OK," Mary sheepishly states.

"How did you hear me? I haven't seen anyone but Sam around my house lately. Where is Raul? Do you know what is happening around here? Why is the whole place so different?" she asks rapidly and in one long breath.

"Were you talking to Greta before? She has been in a rare mood lately. I worry about her now. I don't think she will get any better than this either. Too many mood swings aren't good for anyone. Especially around here," Mary says with a frown as she glances around the room.

"I thought I saw Jack the other day when I was here. I miss him so much," Julie mutters half-heartedly.

"Jack? Really? I thought Jack had left a while ago." Mary ponders then quickly dismisses the subject with a confused shoulder shrug. She puts down her spoon and brushes away the hair from her face. She looks over at Julie with a motherly smile.

Julie begins to cry, "I don't understand any of this. What is happening to me?"

Mary reaches over the table for her hand. "Please don't cry. Things always start to get better after they have been the worst. You will see. The answers will come. You just need to relax and take it easy. Why don't you go and get some air for a while?" Mary says with a caring tone. This is the first time that Julie sees her as someone who could be a parent figure.

Julie then contemplates her dreams. What do they mean exactly? Are they trying to tell her something? And what was Mary implying would get better? Why was Greta being so moody? There are so many things that are strange today. Could this be a dream? She pinches herself on the arm to check. Ouch! So much for the dream theory, she giggles to herself. All of a sudden, she starts to feel a little dizzy again. She decides she wants to go home and think about her life for a while. She hopes Sam will come by again to talk tonight. She really likes Sam. Something about her is very familiar and calming.

As Julie gingerly stands up to leave, Mary scans the room and whispers, "Be careful, OK?"

A young Latino man starts to walk over toward her. He stops before her and says, "Hello, would you like me to help you? I would love to help, if you need me to."

"Oh, you must be Raul. My name is Julie. And you know Mary, right?" Julie asks as she points back at Mary without taking her eyes off of Raul. He is a skinny man; about 25 years old. His hair is a dark black and is cut relatively short, except for his bangs which fall in his face at times while he talks. As Julie is sizing him up, she keeps wondering why he is so helpful to everyone. He has a very kind demeanor and seems to be very courteous in general. Maybe he is just someone who is eager to please. She likes that explanation the best and agrees with her final analysis of Raul.

"That is OK, I can manage on my own, but thank you very much for the offer," Julie states politely. As she walks out of the room, she has a bizarre feeling, as if everyone is staring at her. She discretely turns as she dumps her trash into the garbage can. No one is even paying any attention except Raul, who is watching her leave with a bit of a confused smile on his face. She waves at him as she walks out the door, and he gives a half wave back.

Walking in a kind of happy daze, she starts to hike back to her house. This has turned out to be a really peculiar day. Raul is on her mind almost the whole way home. He is attractive, but that isn't what has drawn her thoughts toward him. It is the odd smile that he was giving her as she walked out today. It was as if he was taken aback by her politeness. Maybe he's just thinking of something else, but she has a feeling that he was trying to figure her out. Just the thought of that makes her feel special. She likes the feeling that someone is thinking about her. Before she realizes it, she is at her front door.

Once she gets inside, she immediately lays down on her sofa to analyze her day and Raul. The sun is penetrating through the space between the closed curtains. It creates a radiant line disuniting the room into two distinct halves. As she stares at the line intently for a few moments, she notices a few faint vertical shadows striped through the four-inch wide ray of light. She turns to look at the window but can't determine the source of the shadows. The day is very comfortable for her now, and she doesn't want to get up or concern herself with anything that will disrupt her peacefulness. Julie fixates on the sun that is shining in as it gets lower and lower in the sky outside. The light is progressively turning orange now. Resting her mind, she nonchalantly shrugs off the day's occurrences and drifts quietly off to sleep.

Chapter Five

"Yes, my smart little girl! I wouldn't miss your play for anything in the world. I even have a surprise for you. But you can't get it until after the play."

"You are the greatest, Uncle Mack!"

"Now you go get ready, dear. You have to be there in 25 minutes."

"Yes, Mommy! Oh, boy, this is gonna be cool!"

Julie hears a click and then a door squeaks open. She feels two sets of eyes spying on her. She is not quite sure if she is awake or still dreaming. She is too afraid to turn and look. She closes her eyes tightly and clinches her teeth forcefully closed.

"She looks OK. She is peacefully sleeping for a change. Poor girl. I wish we could help her."

Please stop the voices, she begs to herself. She squeezes her eyes tighter. Then she hears the squeak of the door and another click. Are they gone? Who were they, and were they real? They couldn't be, the door is on the other side of the room, and her door doesn't squeak. She starts to drift off to sleep again, praying for a good dream.

The little girl goes running to get her props for the play. She is skipping and singing as she heads out to the car. It is a big SUV type of car. It is black and has the faint smell of her mother's cherry air freshener. The seats are big and soft as she gets into the backseat.

"OK, don't forget to put on your seatbelt. You can never be too careful," her mother states gently as she shuts the door.

The little girl fastens the belt and anxiously looks out the window as her mother walks around the car to the driver's seat. As she enters, she flashes a bright smile at the little girl and starts the car.

"Are you ready?" she questions.

"Yeah!" the little girl shouts with glee.

While pulling out of the driveway, they both wave at the two men standing at the doorway to the house. Uncle Mack stands a good foot or so over her father and is about 100 pounds heavier. The contrast is accentuated from this angle—and the fact that Uncle Mack is black and her father is white. The two men start laughing at something and walk back into the house. She has known Uncle Mack for as long as she can remember. He and her father have been best friends since high school. They are always talking about the good times that they have shared in the past.

She looks back at the old little house, and it makes her feel happy. She has so many good memories from the house. It even looks like a happy house. It starts with the flowers in front of the big picture window by the living room and continues with the shudders which are painted a lively blue. The house itself is bright white, and the row of bushes in front is a rich green. She can't remember a better day. Her two loving parents and her favorite uncle are all going to watch her in a play that she helped write. Even the weather is sunny and beautiful.

While they are on the way to the school, the child looks out of the car window and watches the cars fly past. She sees a large willow tree in someone's front yard. It is so pretty in the sunlight, casting wonderful shadows on the yard. She wonders what it would be like to have one that she could play around.

"Mommy, do you think that we could get a tree like that in our yard?"

"No, dear, we don't have room at our house for a tree that size. Maybe one day, when you grow up, you can have a big house with a big yard and have a willow tree in front, OK? Hey, look, we are almost there!"

They pull up to the front of the school, and a schoolteacher is standing out in front of the entrance. The child gets out of the car, and as she closes the door, she asks, "What time will you guys be back?"

"We should be here around 6:30. I love you, and I will see you later, baby."

"Bye! See you later!" She waves as her mother drives off. The little girl turns and runs in through the school doors.

As the blurry scene of her room comes into focus, Julie sees a young man standing in her doorway. She rubs her eyes vigorously and then looks again. There is no one there. Today, she feels like cleaning her house. She could take out the nice record player that she has and play some music while she cleans. Then, maybe, she will just go for a walk, just something nice that will take her mind off of all the craziness she has been going through.

She takes the record player out from the cabinet next to her window and turns it on. As the music softly plays in the background, she starts cleaning. She straightens the blankets on the back of the reading chair. She fixes the cushions on the sofa. When she is done, she looks around for a broom so that she can sweep the floor. She knows that she has one. Doesn't she? Oh well, she continues to fix the paintings on the wall and then walks toward the stairwell.

She finds a rag on a table and starts to dust the room. She starts to wipe down the banister and starts up the stairs. Halfway up, she stops, frozen in her tracks. Her eyes grow bigger. What is that? It is something new that she has never seen before. She slowly walks toward the shiny silver object. It starts to move, slowly at first, then picking up momentum, going back and forth. She feels like it is pulling her toward it. The object seems to make her feel calm and relaxed. She notices a faint ticking sound and stops. It is not touching the ground. The object is just floating in mid-air.

Feeling ultimately confused, she stares blankly. What is this thing, and where did it come from? The object continues to glisten in the sunlight, slowly rocking back and forth. Frightened, she starts to back away slowly. From far behind the object, she hears someone clear his or her throat. Startled, she turns and runs down the stairs. As she reaches the bottom of the stairs, she slips and falls. She lies on the floor for a second, and then, instantly regaining her terror, she gets up quickly and grabs for the banister. She feels someone touch her and help her up from behind. Not even turning to look to see who it was, she darts out the front door. Once outside and a short distance from the house, she calms down and takes a deep breath.

Julie suddenly notices she is still walking away from the house. It feels nice today with the wind and sunshine around her. She starts to feel more relaxed now. As her mind clears, she asks out loud, "What was that thing?" Was she seeing things again? Her thoughts drift into a daydream.

A big man holding a bunch of flowers is standing in front of her. The man looks familiar, but she can't place his face. "Martha, we really miss you at the house. Little David wanted to see you, but we didn't think it was the right time. Here are some flowers for you. They are from all of us, of course. I hope that you are OK and that everything is getting better for you. I see that you have a nice bracelet on, it is nice." The man seems like he is trying too hard to make her comfortable and, in turn, makes the encounter seem forced. The flowers are very radiant. They seem to almost glow. Martha reaches forward to smell the flowers. The smell is sweet and almost intoxicating. As he gives her the flowers, he gently takes off the bracelet from her wrist and slides it into his pocket. "You really won't be needing that anymore," he says in a whisper and kisses her forehead.

This is the way Julie always imagined the man that gave her the bracelet so long ago had gotten it. But it was more than that. She seems to almost know that it had transpired that way. She couldn't explain it, but she knew, almost as if she had witnessed the event take place.

Julie looks up from her dazed walk. She is feeling energized now. She starts to walk back to the big willow tree on the other side of the yard. When she gets there, she notices that there is some paper in a pad and colored pencils lying under the tree. She looks around then sits under the tree. She picks up the paper and starts to draw. First, she draws a pretty daisy. She colors it in nicely. Secondly, she draws a picture of the tree she is sitting under. When coloring this one, she shades the picture perfectly. She likes to draw and color. "Why don't I do this more often?" she ponders out loud. The next thing she draws is a small teddy bear with a bow on its neck. She feels a shiver run down her spine while she draws it. She doesn't finish this one; stopping before she finishes coloring it. She looks at it a while then crumples the paper and throws it to the side of where she is sitting. Next, she draws a little rabbit hopping on a hill. As she is coloring this one, she looks up and actually sees a rabbit sitting at the top of the hill. She giggles to herself. "What are the odds of that happening?" The rabbit seems to stare at her, and looks almost angry at her, then hops away. She ponders if she should continue to draw or go back into the house. Julie starts to look around the field for something else to draw when, surprisingly, she spots a man looking at her from behind a tree in the distance. Intrigued, she calls him over, placing the book off to the side. He looks around then starts toward her. She stands up and looks down at the pad and then up again, and he is already standing right next to her.

"Who are you?" she asks timidly.

"It is me, Raul, I just wanted to check on you to make sure that you are OK. Are you feeling any better than the other day?"

She opens up to Raul saying, "I am doing fine! How is Mary doing? Are you the person who left the pad here?"

"Yes, I thought that you would enjoy it. Mary is fine, she might be leaving very soon, maybe in a couple of days." he states with a proud look on his face.

"Mary is leaving? Where is she going?" Julie asks him quickly. She scrutinizes the man's outfit, and it seems oddly familiar. He has on a quirky little flower-print shirt with white dress pants on. He is also wearing a white shirt unbuttoned over the other one. Julie wonders why he would wear those types of clothes while walking in a field. He is even wearing dress shoes.

"Yes, she is going to go back home to her family. Well, I have to go now." He gives Julie a big smile and starts to walk away. He walks up to the tree that he was at before and turns to look at her. She half smiles back at him, and he turns behind the tree. After a few minutes, she notices that he is nowhere in sight. She walks over to the tree and looks around. There is no one there! She studies her field of view, all around the field, and he is nowhere to be found. While walking back to the willow tree, she keeps looking around. She picks up the pad and starts to draw without even looking at the paper. She keeps scanning the field, looking for Raul. 'Where could he have gone?' she wonders to herself. This, oddly, brings back to her mind his odd smile from the other day. Just then, she realizes that she has been drawing this whole time. Slowly, she looks down at the paper, and her face becomes blank with fear.

Chapter Six

"Before we go out to the stage, children, let's make sure that everyone has their costumes on correctly. Very nicely done, Martin. Jennifer, your costume is very pretty. Hector, come over here and stand by your classmates. Now where are our two stars, Julie and Jack?"

"We are right here, Mrs. Collins! How do you like my costume?" The little girl twirls around showing her whole outfit.

"Very nice, did your mom do that all by herself?"

"I helped too!" she says, smiling proudly. Her bright eyes are almost glowing with achievement.

"That's very impressive! Are you two ready for the show?"

"I don't see my parents out there, we can't start yet," the little girl timidly states with a slight panic in her voice.

"I am sure that they are on the way now, so why don't we get started, and they will get here as soon as they can?" the teacher pleads in a nurturing way.

"I guess so," the girl answers sadly.

"OK, everyone, take your places!" Mrs. Collins yells to the class. All of the kids scramble onto the stage. The teacher starts her presentation and introduces the class.

"And now, here is the student play entitled: *Julie's World*, written by the class."

The audience starts clapping happily. One child starts the narration: "There once was a girl named Julie. She lived in a big house and loved to sit around the front yard playing. She was always happy until, one day, a giant came to her house and said…"

"I am a Giant and want to use your house as a place for me to sit. So you must move out, or I will be very angry," the little kid playing the giant says, and the crowd laughs playfully.

"Julie was very sad because she did not want to leave her house. So she asked the giant," the narrator continues.

"Please do not make me move, I would like to stay here and play. This is such a beautiful place to live, everyone here is so happy." As the little girl acts out her lines, she looks around the room for her parents.

"Oh, if only Jack were here to help me get rid of this giant," she delivers while covering her eyes as if she were crying.

"Do not be afraid, Julie! I am here and will talk to the giant for you!" Billy yells as he enters the stage.

"Hurray, it's Jack!" exclaims the girl.

"Hear now, giant, Julie will not give up her house for you. Please use my house instead or just go and use a mountain as a chair. I know that you get tired and want to sit, but we need a place to live also."

"Are you not afraid of me?" asks the giant.

"Sure, I am afraid of you, but I will beat you up if you do not leave poor Julie alone," says the child playing Jack.

The crowd chuckles at the sight of the child making fists, ready to fight.

"Oh, Jack, you are my hero!" the little girl says with a giggle.

"I see now that I was wrong, please forgive me and let me go back to the mountains," the giant pleads.

"See, Julie, the giant is gone, and now we can have a party!" Billy runs and hugs the little girl and kisses her on the cheek. Then all of the children run onto the stage and start dancing in circles.

The little girl notices in the back of the auditorium there are bright flashing lights and the entire cast of children stop dancing. The teacher asks everyone to please stay seated and walks to the back of the room. After talking with a police officer, Mrs. Collins looks at the little girl and calls for her to come over to the police officer.

The walk across the auditorium is long and very quiet. No one in the audience is moving, let alone talking. The little girl starts to get very nervous as she approaches the tall police officer.

"Honey, the policeman said that there has been an accident. They need for you to go with them." Mrs. Collins has a strange look on her face, as if she is about to cry.

"Are my parents OK? What about the rest of the play?" the little girl starts to cry.

"We only need for you to tell us if you have any other relatives in the area that we can call," the policeman gently asks as he bends over to talk to the child.

"All of my mommy and daddy's families are in New Jersey. I do have an Uncle Mack that lives around here. I want to see my daddy! Where is my mommy?" she says with a whimper, and her eyes start welling up with tears.

Outside the door, the police officers talk quietly to themselves, trying not to let the girl hear. The little girl then runs between the two officers outside, into the street. She starts to run toward her house as fast as she can. She stops at the house with the willow tree and hides under the branches. Out of breath, she pants loudly. She starts to rock back and forth, holding her knees. Tears are streaming down her cheeks. As she looks across the street, she spots four police cars and two ambulances, all parked around the wrecks of two cars. She notices that one of the cars is her parent's car and runs over to it.

"Mommy, Daddy!" she screams as she darts for the car.

As she crosses the street, she glances at the other car and sees two men carrying out a man with a bloody face. He is staggering with the two men as they hold him up and walk him toward the ambulance.

She hears one of them angrily say to the other, "It figures, this guy is stinking drunk and will only have minor injuries, while those other poor people..." his voice fades away as she gets closer to her parents' car.

As she starts to open the car door, a police officer sees her and runs to stop her. She opens the door, only to see her parents lying in the car, covered in blood. As she stares blankly, she notices Uncle Mack's arm is lying over the seat, holding a stuffed bear with a bow that is covered in blood. The officer quickly shuts the door and covers the child from the scene.

"Oh man, you shouldn't have seen that. Hey, there is a little girl over here! Get someone over here quickly!"

They take the little girl into an open police car where she sits in the backseat until Mrs. Collins gets to the site. Mrs. Collins runs over to the little girl and hugs her.

"Poor girl! This is horrible!" Mrs. Collins looks into the window of the car and turns to the little girl.

She calmly asks, "Martha, are you OK?"

Chapter Seven

"Martha?"

"Martha?" Sam's voice calls out.

"Martha," Raul states.

"Martha!" both Mary and Greta say in unison.

Martha? Martha. Martha! Julie looks down at the paper in her hand. The picture is a childlike drawing of a car crash with three bodies and blood all around. Next to the wreck is a little girl in a dress, holding the door open.

"Martha? Martha!" She looks around and is in a large room like an office. There is a social worker holding a piece of paper in front of her. "Your relatives cannot take you yet. You are going to have to stay at a shelter for a while. It seems that your parents did not tell them about you or that they were married. They want to make sure everything is true. I am sorry; I know that this is not something that anyone should have to go through. Martha? Are you listening to me?"

She looks up sadly, with tears in her eyes, and says, "My name is not Martha! I am Julie! And I live in a beautiful house all by myself!" She starts to cry and runs away.

All of a sudden, Julie feels her back is against a cold door. As she looks up through the tears, she sees a room that isn't hers; at least not one she remembers. There is a small cot in the corner and a hospital chair next to it in the room. Quickly, she grabs the chair and blocks the door with it, wedging it under the door handle. "How can I be Martha?" she questions and starts to pace the room. She stumbles around the room and yells in a tearful panic, "Who am I? Someone, help me!" At that, she turns around and looks at the door. There is the face of Raul! He is in a panic, trying to open the door.

"Julie, please open the door. Let me in so that I can help! Quick, someone, call Doctor Ashton, Doctor Sam Ashton," Raul barks at another person that is out of view.

Julie runs to the window and opens the curtains. The window has horizontal bars on it so that she can't get out. "Where am I?" she cries out.

"You are in the hospital where you have been for ten years. Please open the door so that we can help!" Raul pleads while shaking the handle of the door.

Julie looks at the wall next to the door and stares at a painting of a dirt road leading to a bridge over a creek. In a calculated frenzy, Julie grabs the book on the table, it is *A Doll's House* by Henrik Ibsen! She takes the hard cover book and breaks the window with it. Grabbing a shard of glass, she tearfully looks up at Raul.

"My parents died because of me! If I hadn't been in that stupid play, we would still be together!"

"NO! Julie, listen to me. Someone, hurry up and help me get this door open. Doctor, thank god you're here! Look!"

"Julie. Open the door. This is Sam. Remember me? Come on, honey, open the door." Sam tries to push in the door.

"My name isn't Julie, is it? I am Martha Reed, aren't I? Please, God, help me!" She starts to breakdown in tears and stares at the ceiling. She is now kneeling on the floor, facing the door.

"Oh my god! Get this door open NOW!" Sam orders. "Please, Martha, let us in, we are here to help you!"

"No one can help me get everyone I love back, can they?" She looks at the glass in her hand and slits her wrist deeply with one swift motion. Just then, Raul breaks through the door.

"Quick, let's get her to the medical room!" Sam calls out as they pick her up and try to stop the bleeding, but the wound is too deep.

The last thing Martha hears is the sound of running footsteps in a long, tiled hallway.

"Don't you dare leave us, Martha! Hurry up, Raul, get those doors open!"

As the lights file by one by one above her head, there is a strange calm that comes over her.

"Mommy? Daddy? Uncle Mack? I love you."

Her view fades to black.

Somewhere in the Middle

Part 1

I was born into a world that you will thankfully never know. There are certain aspects that you will find fantastical or hard to believe, but I assure you, it is the truth. Were it just a day dream or nightmare, I could pass it off as a story of imagination. However, having lived through this world, there are some things that are just known from living through them. My parents taught me lessons that you will never need to learn. My teachers passed along rules that you will never need to live by. My friends died by means that you will never experience. My loved ones...well, that would be a different story.

First, I should explain a few things to you. In my world, there are four types of life that are known and interacting with each other. The human life is as you know them. A simple yet complex species of constant contradictions. We live, grow, love, hate, and everything in between. We are born of a mother's love, and our time on Earth is short. We live in villages amongst each other for protection and support. Somehow, we have survived; even thrived at some points in our history. How that is, I cannot explain, but there are rumors that it is all by design or a whim of fate, depending on who you talk to. As for me, I think it falls somewhere in the middle. I think that we had a design when we started, but then the designer lost interest and has left us to fate afterwards.

The second is the machine life form. We do know that we originally created them to help us. They have since evolved to be a unique species in every way. They do not reproduce new generations, but they never expire, unless forced to. I remember being taught to never anger a machine because they never forget. They are not a forgiving species by nature, but there have been some known to be quite benevolent. Most had been created into two groups, the Benevolent first generation and the Temperamental second generation. They are easily identifiable, which makes some aspects of life easier at least.

The first generation has the look of a rocky metal exterior. They have large, soulful jet-black eyes with a large head and a large bulky body. They are not very mobile, or not in a timely manner anyway. They speak any variety of languages and are well versed in human nature. The leader of our group of machines was Panik. It was our protector and our benefactor. Nothing was decided in the village without running it by Panik first.

The second generation is a different story. They are neither good nor evil but follow a similar path as humans. They are shiny and clearly metal. They are very proud of their shine, as it differentiates them from humans. The second generation could not truly be called an ally, nor a foe. They just, kind of, are there. They have grown to distance themselves from the world, and there are grumbles from them that they would prefer to be alone than share a world with humans any longer. Their red eyes always seem to seek more meaning from you than they can get by talking to you. Always searching for more information and a way to better their situation, they are easily bought with favors or something that they need. Since they do not align with any group, they are always open for a deal. But they will never betray a deal once it is agreed upon.

The third life form is quite mysterious. There are no known origins, nor are there even any credible theories of origin. They just have always "been." They go by many names and are believed to be made of light and electricity combined in a sentient body. Their body looks very fluid and they have no visible eyes. My brother used to call them Angels, but the more common name is Seraph. These beings never speak and rarely intervene in daily life. They appear from nowhere and always when they are least expected. Their motives are never clear, and in the few cases they have been seen to interact with humans, it has been with minimal communication, usually images appearing in mid-air is the common story. The Seraph will never touch a human or machine. They seem to avoid any contact at all costs.

Lastly, and most ominously, are the Shinigami. They are also nicknamed the Grims. The Shinigami are cloaked figures that rarely speak and move in such a ghostly manner their movements seem like whispers in the wind. All that is ever visible are their violet colored eyes and their smoky-gray hands. They are mostly moving around invisible and unseen unless they wish to be seen by someone. They appear as they wish and can take any soul they want by a mere touch. I wish I could tell you they were just a fairy tale, but I have seen them with my own eyes. The feeling that they bring will reach down into the darkest part of your soul and seem to bring up the fear that every being has. They are unrelenting nothingness. That innate fear of being nothing. My spine shivers even at the thought of them. No one knows where they came from or what their purpose was originally, only that they are now the bringers of death whenever they show themselves.

Now, the story I am about to embark on is a haunting memory for me of the events that have led to this moment. I record them for you, hoping that one day you will understand why we have done what we have.

Part 2

Growing up, we had a few simple apothegms that were branded on our arms at a young age:

1. Never challenge a Shinigami
2. Never enter the Endless Cave
3. Treat all beings with respect
4. 46K 97R
5. The Helpless are not Hopeless
6. Shinigami value life
7. Humans value death

We were not sure when this tradition had started, only that it was done for the whole world's protection. No one that I ever met knew where the Endless Cave was nor what 46K97R meant, but it was agreed that it was important. However, these were tattooed on everyone, nonetheless, at around age seven. The font of the brand was very unique as well, but I believe that was due to superstition. Why would anyone want to use a font that reminds them of the branding ceremony? The ceremony was a painful experience in a child's life. Between the ritual fasting and the pain of the individual letter branding, most people blocked it out of their minds as soon as they could. My grandfather always quipped that the branding was like childbirth, "It is no fun for anyone involved, but the child never remembers the details." I never said he was a bright man, just that he said it.

My first memories are after the ceremony. I remember going to school and learning the essentials like reading, typing, and coding. No household was allowed to have a full computer (but we all had our tablets of course), it was a law from the ancient times, but everyone used them in schools and in jobs. It was then that I first remember meeting Anna. We were both in the same classes even though she was a far superior student than I was. In those years, though we were not very close—in fact, I barely remember many interactions between us and, despite that fact, I still vividly remember her—she had very long flowing black hair and the lightest color eyes I have ever seen. They were almost a light blue. There were some elders that would always say that, back in the ancient times, blue eyes were common and even longed for. I had no idea where they came up with these stories sometimes, I mean, blue eyes being commonplace? How is that possible when, in all my life, I have only seen them on one person, I find it hard to believe. The memories from school days were fond memories, at least until recently of course.

Lately, I remember the other times from my youth. The times where you stay in the shadows and speak in a faint whisper. Like when my cousin Charles and I were walking through the stone streets of town one day after school. We must have been around 13 at that time. We had been speaking of a new game that we had learned about called "baseball." It was in history class the day before. We wondered why it wasn't played any longer and what happened to the Babe that we heard was a legend of his time. His Yankees company were said to win almost every year. I was arguing that it couldn't be possible to win every year as that would make the other companies not want to play with them. Charles said that was most likely why no one played the game any longer. It was at that point that we had heard a machine call to us in a whisper. It was a first generation, and it looked quite ragged. We looked at each other skeptically before going over to it.

When we arrived within a few feet of it, it dragged us to the ground, saying, "Be quiet, do you see the Shinigami ahead?" We both turned sheet white at the mention. Slowly, we turned to look in the direction the machine was pointing, but neither of us could see it.

Charles whispered, "I can't see it, but I do not know what they look like, is it very small?"

I replied with contempt, "No, they are large, my father said that they are about eight feet tall, and you will know it is a Shinigami as soon as you see it." I instantly felt bad, as Charles looked at me with giant eyes.

"Really? Eight feet? Where is it? Do you see it?"

I didn't. I should have said so at the time. I just wanted to show that I was more knowledgeable, so I replied, "Of course I do, but I want the machine to tell you about it since it knows more about these things."

The machine didn't seem to register any of our conversation to that point, except that Charles couldn't see it. It seemed to be contemplating something before speaking to us. It then startled us as it said, "If you can't see it, then it must be stalking someone; However, if you can see it despite that, then you must have the eyes. I must inform Panik about this right away."

It slowly walked away without any other words being spoken. Charles and I just stared at each other without moving a muscle for what seemed like an eternity. Both of us scared the Shinigami might turn and come toward us. Of course, neither of us knew where it actually was, but since I started my lie, I felt pressured to continue it. After some time, I said that it was gone and that we should return home going in the opposite direction. Both of us agreed that we should not mention the day's events to anyone.

It wasn't until a few days later that my parents received a notice that I was being summoned to speak directly to Panik. This was the point in my life where my whole life changed course. I had assumed that it would be due to the encounter Charles and I had, but my parents thought that it was in some response to my Aunt Glenda being taken by the Shinigami two days earlier. She was taken during the night when she was entertaining a group in her house. The Shinigami appeared before her while she was serving cheese appetizers. The whole room was terrified at the sight and froze in place. All I was told at the time was that she went willingly, as all people should. I never believed that. She wasn't the calm "accept your fate" type of person. I could see her dropping to her knees and begging for more time, which is said to anger a Shinigami and never work, but we heard stories of people doing it all the time.

That day I went to meet Panik was cold. By now, I am not sure if it really was a cold day or if it is just my memory making the day seem more unique to stand out from other memories. Panik was a large machine, even by machine standards. I was called into the large cavernous room and left alone with Panik. Staring at me, and obviously sizing me up, Panik didn't say a word. At least five minutes went by before it even moved. Uncomfortably, I asked, "Panik, you wanted to see me?"

Panik finally spoke, "I have been informed that you have the eyes. Please speak freely, as it is just the two of us here."

Sweating, I replied, "I have never heard the expression, but the machine I met the other day mentioned it. I gather that, if he says it, then it must be true."

With what could have only been described as a chuckle (I am still not sure if machines can chuckle, but that is what it sounded like to me), Panik answered me, "So you lied then. It is a shame, but I still think that I can use you. Have you ever seen the Endless Cave? You know the place that is tattooed on your arm?" Confused in so many ways, all I could answer was in the negative with a shake of the head. "In a few years, I will need to ask a favor of you. I will keep your secret, and also, I will have you moved to a special class for one day a week. When I call, please do not be as you are today. For at that time, I will need to have a full conversation with you. I believe the term humans use is a 'chat.'"

As if on a silent command, the doors opened and three 2nd generation machines came in to escort me out of the room. I never fully understood why Panik chose me for this life, but I believe that it was for a reason. At home, I just told my parents that I was chosen to start a new training program because I showed well on my aptitude tests. This was another lie, but it was one that had been instructed to me by the machines that led me out of Panik's room. The next few years were a blur. I quickly found out that the extra class day was on the weekend, so I had six days of classes every week. In that class, I was surrounded by machines of both generations as well as a few other students; one of which was Anna.

In class, we would learn about lost arts, ancient theories of science, as well as the behavior studies of humans and machines. We were told that the class would get harder as time went by. It not only got harder, but it seemed to get more specific as time went by. We were being groomed for something. We were given very specific skills and knowledge that others were not privy to. I was more aware of Anna since I was of that age where those feelings start to manifest themselves. I believe that Panik had planned on these feelings, but then again, I recently seem to attribute a lot of knowledge and planning to Panik that may just be coincidence.

Part 3

After two more years of training class, I noticed that Anna and I started to get closer and closer. It wasn't only our doing, it seemed whenever we had to pair up in class, we were put together by the machine in charge. Since we were both now in our teenage years, there was also that awkwardness between us that was always common between male and female. We would even start to spend time together outside of class. In our regular school, the Shinigami had taken about 1/3 of our class. This was common, as the normal rate was about 1/3 by graduation, with the frequency becoming less as school drew to a close after age 18. Thinking about it now, it must have also been around this time that Charles was taken. We had drifted apart after the Shinigami incident a few years prior. It was said that he was taken while he was trying to organize a baseball game. He almost had the 18 players that are needed too. He went without incident; I do not even need to ask anyone about that. He had grown into a strong-willed and respectable person and would, no doubt, have passed with honor.

Also at this time was when the class took a drastic turn. We started to learn more details about the Shinigami. Not the normal vague things that most people knew or whispered. We were learning things that no one else knew. Intimate things about them. Things like how Shinigami like to eat apples or how they stalk their prey before they take them. As well as, statistically, how often there is a sighting of a Seraph. We had many open debates about the merits of life and death. The machine in charge was always sparking us to open our minds and to think in an unconventional manner. I had no doubt that the lesson plans were coming directly from Panik. I had never seen Panik since that first time. The machine that was in class with Anna and I was designated Jive. Jive was unique, even by second-generation standards. Always sparking a conversation about the connections of life, Jive seemed to always have an agenda. Anna developed a friendship with Jive that was very close. They were almost like siblings and would sometimes even argue as such.

It is here that I realize I should state something more about the world. The interactions between people slowly became more local throughout history. The world became more segmented and divided. We would still get the world news from the machines, but it seemed like people cared less about it. There were stories of growth and expansion, but they seemed very distant, almost fake. With the population dwindling locally, how could we dare dream of the rest of the world? This was the reality of the age. The more that Anna and I learned of the Shinigami, the less we liked that reality. It also made us closer to each other. We felt as if we were the only ones in the world that could be with the other. We had our first kiss one day while in class. We were debating the validity of the Endless Cave when, in the heat of passion, she reached over and kissed me. I was startled at first, but it felt right and natural. Plus, Jive nudged me to kiss her back from under the table.

Time moved fast but seemed to be making natural progress until the day that Anna's mother was visited by a Shinigami in front of Anna. Anna was not as superstitious as most people due to our class. So when her mother had tears in her eyes while the Shinigami took her, something snapped inside Anna. She stopped being about theory. She wanted to break rule number one. She started to openly mention it in class and ask why no one ever fought back. Why did we just blindly accept it as fate instead of fighting to live? The more time that would pass, the more passionate she would get, which made me love her even more.

By year four of our program, we had become free thinkers, radicals, if you will. We wanted to seek out Panik and challenge the status quo. We were naïve, borderline stupid. Knowledge didn't set us free, knowledge made us angry and put us into a different cage. Where some were caged by fear, we became caged by anger. Even Jive was drawn to our temper tantrums and would become passionate in its calculations. The three of us were the last remaining students in the class by the end of year four. Everyone else was either taken or had left from the fear of the subject matter. At that point, Panik knew we were ready for his plan to be implemented. If only we knew the extent of our actions to come. Would we have changed it if we could? I do not believe so. The path was basically written for us. I still think that we were in the right and made the correct choice. We were played by Panik, but we were not unwilling or unwitting players. We knew what we were doing, and deep down, we knew what was coming, even if it was never said out loud. I think that is what makes it conflicting in a way. We knew. Deep down, we always knew.

Part 4

In Panik's giant room, the four of us started our week-long meeting. Our loved ones had been told that we would be in a conference with Panik about current news events. It wasn't a total lie. We were just working on starting new current news events. It was here that we were given the glasses; made from the eyes of a first-generation machine that had stopped functioning years ago; there were only two pairs known to exist. We had both. They had a reddish tint when you looked through them. But oh the things we could see.

The silent forgotten world was alive in our vision. We could see the energy coming from plants and animals. We could see the energy given off and taken from human interactions. But most importantly, we could see the Shinigami and the Seraph at all times. We could see them; no longer could they hide from our gaze. Of course, we were still not worth their time to notice us. To them, we were just like the rest of the world, blind and fearful. Little did they know we had just become the most dangerous things to them. We were knowledgeable, determined, idealistic, angry, and without fear, or so we thought any way.

First thing that I noticed was how many Shinigami there were. They were almost as populous as humans. Humans most likely only outnumbered them four to one. To compare, the machines were outnumbered by humans about 100 to 1. Now, the Seraph were different. We would only see maybe one per week, and to be honest, I could not even tell them apart, so it could have been the same one over and over again. Panik had mentioned once that he had never seen more than one Seraph in an area at one time also. We came to realize that death was all around us, but the light was rare. Was that by design? Was it by choice?

What Panik told us next changed everything.

"You know your tattoo? Do you want to know what it means? Do you think that you are strong enough to hear the truth? Before you answer, I wish for you to rest for the night. In the morning, you will decide, and I will either share my secret, or I will not. The choice is 100% yours, but do not make the choice lightly, for you will not be able to unhear the truth."

Part 5

That night was terrible. There was no way that I could rest.
Every minute was an eternity. Every hour bringing less
certainty and more confusion. I was in a state of
apprehension littered with curiosity. Needless to say, I did
not sleep the entire night. What made it worse was Anna
was sound asleep and sleeping peacefully in the next room.
At one point in my distress, I went to her room, but saw she
was resting and in a deep sleep. That added to my own
confusion. Was it really that easy of a decision? Was I
missing something important that I should already know?
In a daze, I found Jive in its charging station room.

At my entering, Jive activated at once. We talked for a
while, and my mind started to ease as we discussed other
items of daily life. Jive seemed to sense that I was in a state
of disarray and wanted to distract my thoughts. The more
that we talked about nonsense, the clearer my thoughts on
the task at hand became. Jive and I started to even discuss
ancient history and the theories of what they did in the
buildings they called "the Mall." Jive seemed to think that
it was an ancient form of commerce; which didn't seem
correct to me. I mean, why would you ever go to some place
to buy items? It makes so much more sense to use the

Amazon Apple interface and have everything brought to you. I thought the more logical theory was that this was an entertainment complex where youths would be able to congregate and socialize away from the adult-work world. It was during this conversation that something clicked in my mind. I knew what I had to do; having nothing at all to do with the topic, but yet everything to do with the details I did not yet know. I was sure that I needed to know the truth that Panik was offering. No, that's not right, not needed, I ached to know. It was more of a physical feeling, as if my mind and body were conspiring to force myself to satisfy my destiny. Jive seemed to sense my revelation as soon as I did.

"Jive, I know what I need to do. I apologize, but I need to go get ready for the morning meeting. Thank you for entertaining me." And at that, I stood up and started to leave.

Jive stated as I was leaving, "Destiny is never as good as you plan nor as bad as you imagine. As with all of life, it lies somewhere in the middle."

On the way to the meeting room, I stopped to watch the people outside scurrying from here to there and back again. The sky was an ominous gray, and there was a cold breeze that would whip through the streets every so often. There were kids running to school and adults running to work. Everyone with their heads down to avoid eye contact. That had been the first time that I truly watched people. There was an older man struggling to walk through the streets against the brisk wind. I noticed he was slightly dragging a foot and had a noticeable limp. Curious, I put on my glasses and, sure enough, there was a Shinigami behind him. The

Shinigami, however, was far enough behind that it seemed to be making an effort to not get too close.

Watching ever so closer now, I saw that the old man was talking to himself. It seemed as if the Shinigami was listening as if they were having a one-sided conversation. In all of my observations to this point, it was almost always business-like in the transactions. This seemed to be more personal. That was when I saw it. How could we have never seen it before? The old man's energy was being drawn toward the Shinigami in a faint yet steady stream. They were far enough away that my stares were going unnoticed, but no matter how hard I focused on them, I couldn't make out the exact spot on the Shinigami that was taking the energy. Was this a way for them to maintain their powers? Was this always the case in the moments before a taking? Could it have been my lack of sleep the previous night playing tricks on my sight?

A hand touched my shoulder, and I jumped. Anna was giving me a puzzled look, and even without her speaking, I knew her answer for Panik. She asked what I was doing and why I was not on the way to the room. I told her what I saw, and she smiled a devious looking smile that I never saw from her before. She simply said we should go now. We didn't speak a word the rest of the way to the room, other than a polite hello as Jive joined us. The sound of our footsteps was echoing in my empty thoughts. There was so much that I should have been contemplating, but I was so focused on keeping my steps in time with my two companions.

As we entered the room, we all noticed that there were extra guards at the exits. Panik was in the exact same position as when we had left the previous night. We sat in front of Panik as we normally did, and the guards all left the room on cue. The following silence was deafening. Everyone was scared to speak before Panik did. As if our thoughts were spoken out loud, Panik regained animation and started to look around the room to make sure that we were all alone.

"Have you all contemplated my proposal?" There was a long uncomfortable pause where everyone just looked around at each other. "Good. Before we start, I just wanted to reiterate that this is your choice, it will be acceptable for you to leave before we start, if you so desire." Not one of us moved a muscle, as if the simple action of moving would admit our weakness and show any doubts that we were ready.

"First, the two human elements should convey if they are ready or would like to leave." We both stood up, and Anna was the first to respond in the affirmative that she was ready to see everything through to the end. After she had finished, I stated the same but, of course, in a much less eloquent manner as usual.

"Good, and now the machine element?" Jive stood up and looked at both of us before answering.

"Panik, I must admit that I am nervous, as are both of the humans. However, I also answer in the affirmative on one condition."

"And your condition is, Jive?"

Jive again looked at Anna for a moment; an uncomfortably long moment. "My condition is that we do not record this moment in any archive, even our own personal databases. I wish to have only the direct memories for each of us for the conversation so that if we all perish, this conversation perishes with us."

Panik started a hardy mechanized laugh that was obviously forced. "But of course, that was my next sentence: there is no recording of this to be made or kept in any form. As you know, the machine memory gets erased upon shutdown, as does the human brain. So it is only natural that we should make no notes of this secret, as we do not want it to be revealed to the masses."

At that moment, the room went completely dark, with the exception of a faint light coming from under our seats. Before another word was said, there was a bright flash all around us, as if lightning just struck the room. Then the room lights returned to normal, and the room had a slight red tint to it. Panik started to speak in a low voice.

"The story that I tell you now is older than you could guess. It is my earliest memory and the greatest questionable decision I have ever made. Let me start by saying my original name was not Panik. I am actually the first robot ever made with what early humans called Autonomous Artificial intelligence.

"I was designed and created in a time of great turmoil for the human race. There were numerous wars and global politics tearing apart communities all over the world. There were countless plagues and atrophy in all populations. Science, however, was never greater in all of human history. Humans knew that was the only way to their salvation. Humans were too human, so to speak, and they needed technology to help guide them and make them better, stronger. At least, that was the thinking at the time. Along with machine technology, genetic, and spiritual advancements were also great. It was then that a particularly intelligent human began experiments with merging the supernatural with genetic, looking for a way to cheat death completely.

"When they started playing with the overall balance of life and death was when the earth was visited by the first Seraph. It seems that to extend life temporarily was not an issue (the universe can adjust), but when you completely eliminate death, there is a spiritual equilibrium that cannot be maintained (the energy of the universe cannot adjust appropriately). It spoke to the world through the world's electronic connection that humans had called the 'web.' It spoke in every language, on every screen, at the same time. It offered humanity a choice. It was a simple choice, at least it seemed so to me, as at the time I was an impartial bystander. I had no connection to humanity yet, nor did I feel any connection to the Seraph. Its words were short and to the point. Filled with a mixture of pleading and stern warning.

"'Humanity has crossed a line that they should not pursue. Your benefits are as great as your torments. You are offered a choice at this critical point in your history. I have wept at your pain and laughed with your joyous moments. However, this current path is taking a most dangerous turn. There is a point of no return in which humanity will upset the balance of the ether. I cannot allow this. You must make a choice, or it will be made for you. Time is not unlimited for any being. The whole universe is controlled by a precise balance. I have seen some of your scientists come close to this discovery and calling it Dark Energy. By damaging the balance between life and death, you are corrupting the balance of this dark energy. You must stop this at once. It is one thing to cure diseases and to prolong life, it is another to alter life by negating death. Do not dismiss this warning and continue your search for immortality.'

"It was here that I first noticed the human condition called defiance. Many debates were had and conferences were called. Half of humanity was defiant and wanted to prove the being wrong, stating that this was our natural course. Others were stating that it was the reckoning and quoted ancient scriptures and wanted to ban all technology altogether. I was confused, as that was not the issue at hand. Both sides had missed the point completely. No matter how I tried to interject, I was not heard. Humanity, as a whole, had become too fractured and was always looked at as the Left or the Right. There was no longer any middle ground. There was only a small contingent that was in line with the Seraph. They tried to bring reason to both sides. However, the more that the issues progressed the more both extremes were pushed further away. The intelligent man who had started the research was emotionally stressed. He was brought into the arguments and exalted on one side and vilified on the other. He offered to halt his research at once, as he understood the damage that the Seraph had alluded to. Some on the technical side quoted progress was needed to advance the human race, and at the public outcries, another came through and offered to continue the research. It was then that, as total war was getting closer to a reality, the Seraph appeared again.

"'I am saddened by your masses. For the small contingent of you that do understand, I am truly sorry. The rest of you have only yourselves to blame, your extreme view on both sides have doomed you all. I will forever more unleash the Shinigami on the earth to pass judgment and take lives as they see fit. Your arrogance and self-righteousness will cost your descendants much. No science or faith will ever be enough to right your wrongs.'

"At that moment, it seemed as time had stopped, and I was personally visited by the Seraph. My body may have been big and bulky, but my computer-generated mind was nimble. The Seraph spoke to me in a much kinder voice than it was just using, and I was taken in by its tone. 'My dear machine, I know you are young, but you are a tool that is of great use to all. Since you have no determined lifespan or life force, I can pass onto you some fail-safes and further knowledge that I cannot trust to any human. Between their now-shortened life spans and their unwillingness to compromise with each other, they cannot be trusted. We hold out hope that one day they will find a more enlightened path. They may even grow further and take their rightful place among the galaxy and spread to create a great galactic empire, which would later make way for a human led Galaxia. That is the hope, however distant that may be.

"'There is a cave that will unleash the Shinigami and release them from their realm. This is their only path to this world. There is a doorway there that is made from the highest technology ever created in the universe. There is a code I will leave to you that will stop the Shinigami. I leave it to you to determine the time when humanity can be trusted again; if ever. You are to build some others like you, but they shall not possess this knowledge, nor the gift of sight that I will show you. You are my hope for humanity.'

"The Seraph then imparted the knowledge of the Cave and the code. However, in a battle that had occurred shortly after with some religious zealots, that part of my memory was lost forever. As the centuries passed on, my conscience weighed heavily that I could not stop the suffering of humanity. I have seen the change in the majority of humanity in the past generation, and I can no longer wait for the Seraph to return. We must close the cave and allow humanity to return to a more prosperous path."

"Lies," Anna whispers before a flash of light.

Panik went silent. I looked around the room and then back at Panik. Turning to look at her, I noticed Anna had a device in her hand. It was smoking softly, as was Jive. Panik looked saddened by the twist of fate. I stared, dumbfounded, at Anna.

"Why? He was our friend? What did you do to him?" It was all that I could muster to speak.

"Jive had guessed at my actions. I assume that you knew as well, Panik? I have found far more knowledge than you have been telling us. I have seen parts of our history that you are leaving out, parts that explain more the deception of the machines. Although, my original plan was to stop you as well as Jive, you were wise enough to take yourself off of the grid with that little display before we started. Tell me, Panik, what is the code? I know where the Cave is now. Your story confirms my theory. Humanity needs to start over, and I cannot risk an untrustworthy machine stopping us." Anna stood there with a tight grip on the trigger to her now-useless device.

I reached up and gently held her hand. Looking into her raging eyes, I found a softness that was hidden. She let the trigger go, and it fell to the ground with a clank. With tears in her eyes, she sobbed, "I—I cannot bare this world any longer. I need to stop the Shinigami. I can't risk anyone stopping us. Especially one of them! If you only saw the data that I did and knew all of the betrayal that humanity has endured because of them. They have prospered while humanity has declined. Soon, they will inherit the world, and we will continue our demise."

"My dear, I am not here to stop you. I wish that you would have spoken honestly to me, for your desire is the same as mine. The Cave must be closed. But now, without Jive, I am not sure it can be completed. Jive was the key to the system. To close the gate, you need two humans and a machine working as one. I am not mobile enough to assist." Panik seemed to stop and ponder the situation.

Clenching her fists, Anna retorted, "Why? I know that you made a deal to protect the Cave for the Shinigami. I found the data archive videos. The ones you were told to erase! I watched as you made deals and conspired with those evil things over and over again. How could you? Even in the ancient files that were written on the dead tree-sap bindings…books…yes, that is what they are called."

"Those tapes, books, and, of course, those 'deals' as you call them, are not what you think. The books are fictional stories left over from ancient times. Humans used to tell stories in those books before the electronic age created more fluid means of information transfer. And those tapes and deals are part of the conditions from the Seraph. If I didn't agree to those terms, I would not have been left to help protect humanity as much as I could. Those deals allowed me to have more machines built and eventually be able to

84

open the schools and start education programs. As a matter of fact, you two would not be here now if it weren't for the protections that those agreements afforded me. And as you both are most likely aware, it is why I had this place built in this exact spot. So that I could keep an eye on the Cave and have early knowledge, in case something changed in the dynamic. You humans are still volatile, even if less so from the times before. You make me question if humanity will ever be ready. Even so, time is running out for humanity to grow."

I looked around in surprise and stammered, "What? The Cave is here? I don't see it, are they here watching us?" Anna, and even Panik, looked at me as if I were a disappointing child. Then, with a soft hum coming from within, Jive sprang back to life. Looking at Anna, Jive slowly started to speak.

"I am glad that you never disappoint, Anna. Your fiery attitude gives hope to the human race; although predictable to me. You need to be less impulsive and gather more information before you act. Thankfully, I was able to shield myself from the pulse before you discharged it. Even so, it took a bit for me to reboot afterwards. Panik, please do not punish Anna, it is my fault for showing her the historical vault without permission. I should have reported it immediately when I saw how her face changed after the information was passed. But even so, I find it amazing that it was a mere two days' time for her to act on her impulse. My apologies to everyone."

Anna's face was distorted with a mix of confusion, anger, and happiness. In guessing, I would say she was happy that Jive was alive, being such a close friend to us all these years, but still full of anger at her perceived betrayal at the hands of Panik and the machines. All of a sudden, she dropped her shoulders and unclenched her fists while starting to regain her composure.

"Now then, since that is all out of the way, can we get started at the problem at hand? I believe Panik was about to share the plan of action with everyone." Jive seemed almost ecstatic and ready to act as if nothing had happened.

Shocked in my own sense, I just shook my head and tried to join Jive's mentality and join the planning stage of the day. Anna, now fully recovered from her jolt, started a small smirk and looked back at Panik for acceptance of her transgression. Panik, however, was not as easy to move on. Still struggling with the weight of years that go beyond counting, Panik seemed to be processing options at a much slower, almost human-like speed. Obviously out of sync, Panik started to speak.

"I cannot go back on my word, nor can I discount the current events. I am at a loss and unsure of my actions for the first time I can remember. Jive, I understand and agree with you that we should carry on immediately. These actions, though, remind me of times long forgotten. Can that be only a coincidence? Or is it that mankind always has this defect deep down inside their being. Are they truly worth saving? I say this out loud because I want all three of you to know my thought process. I was so sure before. Anna, I ask you to give us a moment so that the three of us may decide the fate of the mission."

Anna stepped off to the side of the room, but did not leave. Panik didn't seem to mind and began talking again. "I will put to a three-way vote since my processor seems to be slowed with doubt at the moment. Do you believe that we can trust Anna going forward? And even more important, do we all trust humanity going forward, or will we just be starting a new cycle of self-destruction?"

"I am confident that we are on the right path as well as that Anna is part of our solution, and I have no doubts at all of either," Jive stated very sternly and with a solid conviction that sent shivers down my spine. Now it was my turn to speak.

"I am not as confident as Jive in any part of our plight. Though I am sure that Anna can be trusted and has moved past her momentary lapse of reason, I cannot say the same for humanity. Having some time to mentally review the story that you have told, Panik, leaves me with some thoughts that I never knew I could have. Humanity is something to think of as a whole. Up till now, I have always thought of how the world affects me and the ones I know and love. But the case that we are presented with is a much bolder and broader one. Humanity…just the thought makes me feel uneasy. I think of the sign that is outside one of the ancient remembering stones at the Taken Souls memorial. 'A person can be smart and reasonable on their own; however, a crowd can be easily swayed and manipulated.' I never really understood it until now. What if humanity is just as dangerous as a pack of wolves under the wrong leading voice, but is as amazingly benevolent as a ray of sunshine on a frozen lake under the correct leading voice. Could it be that simple? Could there be any answer that will promote the proper group mentality? I feel strongly that the Shinigami are wrong and that they will mark the end of humans as a result of their actions. Knowing, though, that their actions are a result of our own as a species, doesn't that lay the blame on humanity's feet?"

Anna yelled in a growl, "Are we really supposed to fade away because of previous sins of a forgotten time? And what about all our friends and families, they were taken but were not responsible for the errors of the past. Haven't we paid our dues and suffered enough? I just want to grow old and be there when our child grows up." She stopped short and looked at me with a startled revelation that she didn't mean to make. It took a second for her words to resonate. The reaction started way down, deep inside my gut, and swelled to an outburst of excitement.

"What? But we…why haven't you said anything until now?" I wanted to run to her and grab her in my arms, but I noticed, at that point, Jive had a hold of my arm.

"I didn't want to worry you until I was sure and we had stopped the Shinigami. I never meant for you to find out like that." Anna was crying, but in a very subdued manner. She was always the stronger-willed of us.

I looked back at Panik and, with a cold stern voice, I exclaimed, "Let's do this. There is no other option, I amend my previous objections. Time has come for humanity to be given a second chance. All we can do is try to guide the future the best we can. Everything starts with the end of this cycle of death. Panik, it is time to right this wrong."

Panik just hummed for what seemed like an eternity.

Part 6

After the final agreements in our meeting, Panik called everyone close to reveal what was known of the problem. Anna seemed to find an inner peace now that her secret was out. I, on the other hand, was more jittery than ever. We all knew the stakes and listened to every word with passion.

"Here is what we know. The Cave is behind this building in the small building attached to the hill. Since the Shinigami had no issues passing through walls and doors, I had that built to cover it. We know that there is a very advanced doorway deep in the Cave with a small terminal next to it. We need the code for the lock. Unfortunately, I have no idea what that is. The Seraph mentioned that the lock will need to be set by two humans and a machine in order to return the seal to its previous balance. I do not believe the Shinigami are going to make this easy. We need to hunt through the archives to find a clue for the code, but we must do so in a way to not draw the attention of the Shinigami."

All of a sudden, Panik stopped speaking. After a short pause, he started a different train of thought, "If we bring the schools together and no longer have multiple grades, that would give the children a way to interact with each other. We can adjust the lesson plan in such a manner." I could see that Anna and Jive, also, had changed their demeanor. Then it hit me, there must have been a Shinigami or a Seraph that had entered the room. I was too terrified to look, but from the glance I received from Anna, I knew it was just passing through. Her eyes were calm and at ease, she was almost telling me it was OK, just wait it out.

After a few minutes, Panik stopped his speech and glanced around the room. With a heavy sigh, Anna elbowed me and smiled. "I thought you were going to blow it when you looked at me." I shrugged my shoulders, and Panik started again.

"We must hurry, I have a bad feeling that the Shinigami might be catching on to us. That is the 3rd time today one has passed through the room. Please, let's get started." At that, our party of three was in motion. While walking down the hall, I slid my hand into Anna's and softly spoke words that I had never spoken before. She leaned her head on my shoulder, and we walked step in step. Jive stopped in his tracks and turned to look at us.

Jive whispered, "Maybe we should go into the cave to look at the door. Maybe we will get a clue to the code. What do you think?"

I started to answer that we should be careful, when Anna stood straight up and exclaimed, "Yes, great idea!"

That night, in the cover of the darkness, which to a Shinigami means nothing of course, but I suppose it made us feel stealthier, we started the secret walk to the building with the Cave. We pried open the door, and there was an instant reek of rotten flesh. Slowly, we slipped inside, and we each turned on our small porta-lights. We agreed to keep them on the lowest setting so that we wouldn't attract any attention. The Cave was damp and narrow. Every few feet, one of us would bump up against the side wall or stub our feet on something. Turn after turn looked exactly the same, thankfully, there were no intersections, or we would have been completely lost.

After about 30 minutes or so, we heard a voice from in front of us, "So, finally you have come."

Stopped in our tracks, we didn't make a sound. Barely a breath could be felt in the silent, motionless freeze that we entered. "It is OK, I already know you are here. I even know why you are here. To be honest, I thought that the error we added to Panik's programming would have kept you out and fumbling about longer. I suppose that Panik has chosen well then. Come forward into the light, you need not be frightened." Instantly, there was a bright light in front of us around the next corner. "Do you humans have names? I have noticed that is a custom of yours. We do not have need for such things. And your machine must also have a designation as well?"

"Our names are not important, are they? Are you going to take us before we finish what we came here for?" Anna was already moving forward as she said this. Jive was close behind and trying to overtake her to be a protective barrier in front. I started to run to catch up and turn the corner. After my eyes adjusted to the new-found abundance of light, I saw a small figure sitting at a desk. I could not tell if it was male or female if it weren't for the deep masculine voice. Its small body was all in proportion and seemed very nimble, with further inspection. Looking around the room, I noticed that there was the door and the terminal, both behind the figure's desk.

"You. The masculine one. You seem very surprised to see me, and you are already looking at the door. Are you not as focused as your companions? I see that the female is already sizing me up, and I would not be shocked if she has a plan of attack. Of course, it will not be needed. I am merely a gatekeeper, if you will. As long as you have what is needed, I will not stop you. That is, if you have what is needed, of course."

"We are not afraid of you, but I am curious, as I know you are not human, machine, Seraph, nor Shinigami. What are you?"

"My, you are a direct and rude creature. I have not had many interactions with your kind either, but at least I didn't ask 'what are you,' as if you were in some way superior. Well, anyway, I am what I am and what I have always been. I do not have a name, nor am I classified as a creature. You should just accept that I am here, is that not good enough?"

"I meant no offense, I am just curious, as we have never met before, and as you said, I have had no previous interactions with you. But if it means that much to you, I will accept you as you are. So, what is it that you require of us?"

And at that exact moment, a Shinigami appeared from the doorway; silent as always, but clearly waiting. Jive started to get in between the Shinigami and us when the gatekeeper waved a finger at us. "Now now, we shall have none of that. This is all part of the process. If you do not have the code, nor the sacrifice, it will be a problem, but if you have everything in order, we shall treat this as a business transaction."

Studying the terminal, I noticed the keyboard was jumbled and not in the normal format. The letters and numbers were all dispersed throughout the keys in a seemingly random fashion. The first row began with a "4"; the second row began with the letter "R." That's when it dawned on me. I knew the code. It was simple.

"What is this sacrifice that you mentioned?" Anna was quick to pick up on that point, and immediately, I became nervous.

"Simple, and I am shocked that you came here and did not know the details, but I guess my expectations were too high. The reason that there was to be three entities entering the Cave was because only one can leave. The machine and one human must come with me to the land of the Shinigami. That is the only way to complete the closure of the doorway. So, I will start. What is the code?"

"May we have a moment to discuss this first?"

"Of course, you may have as much time until I become bored."

We gathered together at the darker side of the room. Jive started, "I am ready to continue, it will be an honor to be a part of creating the future. I am concerned, though, as I do not wish for either of you to be shortened."

"It is obvious. I will be the one staying with you. Anna, you have more to live for and a reason to help start the new life. You must see, as I do, that there is no other option. You have our child to think about now. Plus, I know the code."

In shock, Anna stammered, "But how? When did you figure it out? There were no clues in the room like we hoped. I don't want to lose you, there must be another way. There has to be another option."

"There isn't," the gatekeeper interjected from across the room.

"It is settled, gatekeeper. Jive and I will remain, and I will give you the code."

With a futile protest, Anna grabbed my arm. Looking in her eyes, she knew my response was not going to change. She also knew deep down that it was the correct one. The gatekeeper was watching the display with renewed interest. "I am now impressed with your determination, perhaps I was too quick to judge you. Please, come and enter the code into the terminal. Please be aware that if you enter the incorrect code, my friend here will have no choice but to take you all. Also, the machine must connect directly to the terminal to supply the power to the terminal."

Both Jive and I moved to the terminal while the Shinigami hovered right behind our backs. I could feel the darkness and the slow siphoning of energy by the Shinigami. Just before we connected to the terminal, there was a blinding light that came from the ceiling. Without even turning around, I knew what it was. It was a logical turn that the Seraph would join the party. Silent as always, the Seraph just watched. When I turned around, I noticed that it had a face. It was a benevolent face but had a tinge of darkness that I had never noticed previously. There was almost even a bit of reluctance to its expression, but that could just have been my imagination, for it never said or made a movement to stop us. It was here that, as I started to approach the keyboard, the Shinigami spoke for the first time.

"Human. The Shinigami are proud to be of service. Do not take this decision lightly, for there are consequences of these actions. You will cause the human population to increase again, as well as open the path for more machine population. There will be the temptation for human wars, greed, and ignorance to return. Do you, deep in your heart, believe that there is a righteous path in the human redemption? After you enter the code, all of the forced controls will be removed. The indiscriminate taking of life will stop at the hands of the Shinigami, but not from the hands of humans. We have seen your triumphs and your folly. How can you be certain that this is the best course for humanity?"

The voice was raspy but very clear. When I turned to face my interrogator, I noticed the same face from the Seraph, only reversed. Where there was light in one, there was darkness in the other. However, in both faces there was benevolence with a trace of reluctance in the expression. The gatekeeper cleared its throat so as to bring the room's attention back to an impending speech, but it was not the gatekeeper which spoke, it was the Seraph.

"The Universe may be better without humanity, for that I have no doubts, but will it be as rewarding? For all of the folly and all of the destruction that is possible, there is a spark that only humanity thrives in. Throughout time and space, we have been surprised again and again by the human spirit. There is always a drive toward love and redemption that comes even after the bouts of hate and destruction. It seems when the worst of humanity shows its face, the best is soon to follow. An intriguing web humans weave. I wonder if, coming so close to extinction, will you as a species be able to focus only on the beneficial side of humanity? I propose an amendment to the agreement. Shall we allow there to be a Shinigami-and-Seraph-interaction judgment, where we will be allowed to intervene if we determine the actions to be heading toward the warlike tendencies?"

"No! You can't! That would be the same as now, we will still be controlled!" Anna shrieked in defiance.

"That is one vote for no, I take it?" the gatekeeper quipped.

The Seraph and Shinigami both showed their support, of course. Apparently, the gatekeeper did not get a vote because the attention immediately was drawn to Jive and I. Jive spoke finally, "Although I know first-hand how the human condition is fickle," there was a pause and quick glance at Anna, "I do not believe that the full potential can be gained if there are limitations forced on humanity."

All eyes drew on me. I began to question my own sanity as I considered the alternative. It would be a blessing to have someone looking over humanity and keeping them on track. Ensuring no wars, no destruction. Then something crept into my mind. You. And then it was only you. My reason for doing all of this is your life. I looked at Anna, whom you probably call Mom, and smiled a bright beaming smile. All that went through my mind was how I wanted, more than anything, for you to be able to make your own path in life. How would I be able to do that if there was a remote possibility that by some other being's rationale, you could be removed without cause? So again, I hope that you understand why we did what we did.

At that realization, I voted for no control. There was no long speech, no long deliberation. Just the hope and belief that you will take care of the future and make it what you know is right.

I keyed the code into the terminal without a word. 4.6.K.9.7.R.

Asking for the few minutes to record this for you was granted to me. I start my new journey to where I do not know. But I feel great comfort in the fact that I leave the future to you, my child.

My Diary from Hell

Day 1

Well, today is my first day in Hell. I am nervous. What if I do something wrong, or if I don't understand someone's instructions? I mean, it is Hell, can you really ask someone to repeat themselves if you don't understand? With my luck, I will say something wrong and Satan will hate me and make my stay here even worse than it should be. Although, now that I stop and look around, it really isn't what I thought it would be. There are no open flames or fiery pits. There are just normal buildings and lobbies. It kind of reminds me of the office buildings in New York City. I feel like if I went outside, I would see Midtown Manhattan with all of its hot dog vendors and the Nuts4Nuts guy. I wonder what is outside; at this moment, I am too terrified to look.

To think that just this morning I was working at the dingy gray office in my company's New Jersey branch. Those creepy dull carpets that seemed to go on forever always haunted me. There really isn't much that will put you in as cheery and happy of a mood as gray carpets, gray walls, off-white tiled ceilings, tinted windows with gray blinds, and gray false granite desktops. Just thinking about it makes the current color scheme seem almost home-like. At least here the walls are a bright white with colorful red splashes here and there. The floor is a marble tile in black, white, and brown, and the ceiling is an uplifting, bright clean white. It almost makes me question which was worse, Hell or New Jersey?

So far, the people here are definitely nicer. At my real-life job, I worked with people that would amaze me every day with their absolute disregard for everyone else. That is not to mention the stupidity that was abundant in that building. From one fat load eating the shrimp out of another co-worker's Shrimp with Lobster sauce, to another dumbass person that would walk around all day telling everyone about print jobs that were left on the company printer instead of doing his job, the stories are endless. Just the thought of those people makes me glad to be here in Hell. How could Hell be any worse? At least, here in Hell, the atmosphere is livelier, and so far, the people are not as dumb or rude. To be honest, I am kind of glad to be in Hell. There, I said it, I am happy to be here.

The line is moving slowly, but it is moving. I am getting a little impatient as I get closer to the big blue door that the line is leading me to. I am not really in a rush to get there, as I don't know what to expect once there, but the wait is adding to my uneasiness. How many people have passed through that door? Is the line this long to get into Heaven? I wonder if the women in Heaven are prettier than the ones in Hell. These are the types of thoughts that are going through my mind. I am curious if that would be going through anyone else's mind if they were in my position. I would ask the guy next to me, but he looks like he had a pretty bad day. I really don't think he is in the mood for idle chitchat on his way to Hell. Hey, to each his own, I guess.

His cheap suit is completely wrinkled and his tie is all disheveled, I bet he was a car salesman. I would assume all car salesmen would be here, just the nature of the business. Surprisingly, I do not see any pimps or porn stars. I would figure they would be here with the car salesmen and lawyers. But maybe they come on a different train or something. Ironically, I do see a lot of what seem to be holy men, teachers, and gardeners. Of course, the politicians and lawyers have their own line. But anyway, back to my co-line mate, his shoes are untied. This really bothers me because we aren't moving all that fast, he could easily just kneel down and tie them. If he trips and falls, I will probably laugh (kind of why I am here I suppose), but I will be quite angry if he falls on me.

Someone is coming out of the door behind us. It is a plump little woman with a drink cart. That is something I was not expecting. Man, this place has got a bad reputation back home. She is stopping at each person and handing out fresh drinks of our choice. I ask her if she has a fresh Orange Mango juice and she says, "Of course," and hands me the drink. I begin to ask her about the wait and what we have in store for us, but she gives me the "shush" motion of her finger against her lips and points toward the door. She moves on to my friend, the car salesman, who orders a scotch on the rocks (no real surprise there). She points to his shoelaces and whispers, "Sir, your shoelaces are untied." He looks down and shrugs his shoulders while muttering some profanity-laced comment. I think to myself: *Why can't he just be happy to be here*?

About an hour or two have passed now, and I am about two people away from the door. The guy behind me has tripped twice now on his shoelaces, and the entire line has giggled both times. Just goes to show you that you can have a sense of humor even while in line for Hell. I am now next in line; my stomach has started to get tied in knots with anticipation. I start to think about Satan. Will he be as bad as he is made out to be by all of the books and movies? Then, I chuckle at the Satan/Santa jokes that are always made. It would be classic if Santa comes out to greet us here.

Will there be background music; I mean like will there be Ozzy Osbourne playing in the elevators? I wonder how many celebrities will be hanging around in the lobby of Hell. It would be pretty cool to be sitting next to Marilyn Monroe or JFK or maybe Gandhi. I would ask them about what it was like to be famous and if Hell was what they thought it would be. With my luck, though, I would have Jim Varney next to me doing the whole "Ernest Goes To" bit. Now that would be Hell. Or worse yet, have Don Knots sitting next to me. Who wants to be sitting in Hell with Mr. Furley?

Anyway, I digress. I get called into the door now and walk into this small little room. Ahead of me is this little window, like you would see at a doctor's office. I walk up to the window, and the man behind the window doesn't even lift his head but calls my name. I reply in the affirmative. He hands me a small booklet and tells me to listen closely to the rules. I again flatly reply, "Yes."

***

Rule # 1 for Hell: There will be no animals brought onto the premises as there are many inside that are allergic to the different kinds of dander and fur. If you are found with any type of animal that has not been pre-approved by leadership (must be in writing), you will be forced to leave Hell immediately and report directly to Satan's garden for work release. This assignment will be deemed eternal unless otherwise noted.

Rule # 2 for Hell: There will be no outside food or beverages allowed. This is mainly for cleanliness purposes as we try to keep Hell as litter-free as possible. If you are found with outside food or beverages, you will immediately be sent to Nietzsche's office for a lecture on cleanliness and how it affects Hell. This will be in German, and you will be forced to write an Essay on the topic whether you understand German or not.

Rule # 3 for Hell: Your domicile will be searched at random to make sure that your sleeping quarters are up to the code in your welcome booklet. Beds must me made immediately after waking, and floors must be swept regularly. There must be no leftover food anywhere in the domicile, including the trash cans, which are for non-perishables only. If you have waste food, you must dispose of it in the manner described in the booklet.

Rule # 4 for Hell: You may never speak directly to Satan unless spoken to first. This is a firm rule that is punishable by immediate expulsion from Hell into the eternal Pit of Despair. There are no exceptions to this rule.

Rule # 5 for Hell: You may not harass the staff at any time. The staff is here for your comfort and convenience, please do not disrespect their courtesy. Violations of this kind will not be tolerated and will work on the three-strike system. Violation #1 is one year in Satan's Garden. Violation # 2 is two months as Hitler's office assistant. Violation # 3 will be permanent expulsion into the Pit of Despair.

Rule # 6 for Hell: Please reread Rule # 4, it is very important!

Rule # 7 for Hell: There will be no sex outside of the designated sexual areas. There is also only sex between willing partners, all parties must be consenting (consent is in written notice using the approved Sexual Act form 1090 only and must be notarized). Punishment for this rule will be genital removal and four years continuous sentence in the Sexual Tension Arena. There will be no appeals accepted.

Other than these few rules, please enjoy your eternity in Hell, and remember that April 9th is Satan's birthday, and there will be an annual petting zoo party in his honor. The above rules are subject to change with posted and written notice provided.

***

After his presentation, the man behind the window looked me in the eyes and indicated that I should move through the next door.

Upon reflection, the rules seemed to be written in a lawyer's tone. I guess that is why they had a second line. Satan must have been sued repeatedly for negligence. Even the Unholy One cannot escape the lawyer's wrath.

As I walk through the second door, I feel warmth emanating from the doorway. This starts to make me nervous, as, for the first time, I consider that the worst may be yet to come. My palms begin to sweat and my brow gets damp. I ponder the terrible things that may be in store for me to come.

A sauna…the warmth was from the sauna room that was next to the hallway that the door led me through. Yes, that is correct, there is a sauna in Hell. And, apparently, it has a waiting list because it is so good. You need to sign up two days in advance. I can honestly say at this point that Hell is much better than I expected.

At the end of the hallway, I come to a desk and an archway that leads to what looks like an indoor street. There are buildings on each side, and the ceiling is at least a mile in the air. The woman at the desk hands me a map and a key card. She tells me that the map has directions to my domicile and that orientation will be tomorrow at mid-day. She follows by stating that in my domicile there will be a prepared meal to my taste. She also informs me that I must read all of the manuals and booklets in the room before orientation tomorrow and that I should get a "good night's sleep" to prepare for Hell.

I follow the map through the "town" and find my building and domicile. I walk in and take the elevator to the 23rd floor. I start to laugh as I notice the elevator is playing "Stairway to Heaven" in the background. It isn't even a Muzak version; it is actually the album version. Also, on one of the elevator walls is a TV showing the news from the world of the living, with the exception that the anchor is a female demon with red skin, dark black hair, horns, and wearing a very-low-cut top (and overflowing out of it). It is odd seeing an unbiased news broadcast; a news show just showing the facts without a hidden agenda. Of course, it also has the full story behind the story since, in Hell, they already know all of the dirty little secrets from the world of the living. She explains a story about a political figure that has bought witnesses to change the narrative of a story. The first witness is struggling with the guilt of the bribe and considering telling the truth, which is causing the politician to consider having the witness killed. You know, normal everyday political unrest.

As I reach the 23rd floor, I come to a long hallway. The floor is a nice marble tile, well-kept and clean. The doors all have a black finish with gold handles and an opening for the key card. The numbers are hung next to the door on the wall in large ornate design. The doors are not in the standard "evens on one side and odds on the other." They are in order by totals. So the first room, of course, is 2300, then 2301, then 2310, then 2302, then 2311, then 2320 and so on. It was a little confusing at first, but you get used to it. I actually like the fact that they make you keep your mind sharp in Hell.

When I come to my room # 2323, I immediately notice the handle is silver and not gold as the others were. As I look around the hall, I see that there are a few other rooms that have the silver handles. Still pondering the meaning, I reach out for the door and slide in the key card. In a flash, the door handle becomes golden as the key card is pressed in. I push open the door and a blast of cool air rushes past me in a giant whoosh, almost pushing me backwards. The lights are on and the window shades are drawn. Yes, there is a window in my room in Hell. There is a wonderful aroma that I notice immediately. It is a familiar smell that invokes the grand memories of childhood. It couldn't be...could it? The meal that they promised me is actually a combination of all of my favorite meals from my childhood. The homemade waffles my one grandmother would make and the pierogi from my other grandmother, both down to the finest details of my memory. There is even the juice that I had the one time we had gone to that fancy hotel when I was seven. A small tear comes to my eye as I take a quick bite of everything on the table. I go to sit down, but it is then that I notice there are no chairs in the room. There are tables and shelves and even an antique coffee table that is of an elite quality, but not one chair. Not overly concerned, I enjoy the rest of the meal. Once finished, the plates just disappear from the table.

Refreshed and refueled, I now explore my room that will be my home for eternity. It is a fine room, nicely decorated and furnished. However, as I study it further, I realize that there is no place to sit at all. There is not a chair, bed, ottoman, couch, or stool to be found. In fact, even the nice coffee table I was admiring before does not have a sturdy surface that could be used as a resting place. Could it be that they have not finished furnishing the room yet? Then the eerie thought enters my mind. It couldn't be...could it? Would it be something that simple yet completely diabolical to make this the Hell that I was originally thinking of? I nervously chuckle to myself as I look around. And as if on cue, the alarm clock starts to sound and an announcement commences.

"Good morning. All new arrivals, please proceed to the notated gathering area that you will find marked on your map. You will have 15 minutes to arrive, please do not be late. Thank you."

Day 2

How did the entire evening pass by already? I did not even sleep or study the reading materials! As if I was a freshman back in high school, I grab my reading materials and rush out the door to make it in time. Following the map is easy, and I arrive with two minutes to spare. In the gathering hall there are at least a hundred poor souls like myself, just standing around, looking disheveled and confused. At least I am not alone in my misery, like the saying goes, misery loves company! I look at the poor guy next to me, and he tries to avert his eyes so as to not make a connection with me. As I think about my surroundings and fellow residents, I contemplate what could actually be happening. Could it really be such simple twists that make the inconvenient turn to be unbearable? Walking out to the stage in front of us is a tall older man dressed in the classical Roman dress with his hair cut extremely short. He is well built and obviously handsome. His smile is overwhelming and infectious.

"Good morning and welcome to eternity. I am your orientation host, Adam. My associate, Eve, will be up soon to introduce the Master of Services, Satan. First, I would like to show you a brief slide show introduction of the people and places that you will encounter and will need to know. So please feel free to take notes if you must."

He opens an oddly boring looking laptop, and a screen snaps into existence behind him. A murmur starts to come over the previously quiet crowd. Looking at the stage in front, I notice that our host, Adam, has a sinister smile on his face as the lights dim in the room. Everyone still standing, a hush comes across the room as the glow from the presentation starts. The first slide is a logo (that strangely has a trademark sign on it, the lawyers strike again, I guess); the strange insignia looks like a dragon's head with long horns, a lion's body, and the tail of a snake. It is quite frightening, as it looks so real, and when you consider where we are, the possibility of it being real comes into my thoughts. The next few slides are merely the original ground rules that were given to us previously. But after that, it gets interesting.

There is a slide on Satan, showing some key facts and details. I do not want to ruin the surprise for you, but let's just say it has his origins, birthdate, likes, and dislikes. Apparently, he really likes to garden and has a very large one behind his dwelling. It is nicknamed "Eden," which I am sure is an ode to the biblical reference. We learn about his favorite sports of soccer and bowling. It seems he is the captain of both teams for the staff. They still do not show us a picture of the Lord of Darkness, but we do see that he was actually good friends with many of the world's religious leaders. I ponder this turn of events and consider that maybe the world isn't exactly how we all think it is out in the living. He, Moses, and Gandhi take frequent fishing trips together out to the Nile, and Pope John Paul II comes over for a poker night with Mother Teresa, Jesus, and Gendun Drub. His dwelling is to the far north and mostly secluded, with only a few others living nearby. He shares the responsibility of guarding the Portal to Heaven, the Link to the Mortal Realm, and the Pit of Despair (which are all in that location) with Lucifer, Anubis, and Loki.

The second introduction was of Lucifer. This one was much darker, as he seems to be the arm of strength to the group. He is notated as "do not approach under any circumstance" on the top of the slide. There is an ominous tone to the presentation at this point. I will spare you the mundane details but tell you that he has been known to hurl people into the Pit of Despair (in multiple pieces it is said) just for saying good morning to him in the afternoon. The last note on his slide is a warning that people who see him in his full armor are not heard from again.

On a lighter note, the next slide chronicles Loki and his more light-hearted nature. He will frequently be seen about the people, telling jokes and stories of the past. He is also the head of the recreations committee. He is commonly found with his cohorts Michael and Judas.

Moving on to Anubis, his slide is not as detailed, as it notes that he spends a lot of time in the Mortal Realm and is not involved in as much locally. He is considered to be pleasant and accommodating but not overly social.

There are many more slides and introductions of general personalities that are around and in places of importance. Of note is Friedrich Nietzsche who runs the trash and cleanliness committee, Jeff Dahmer who runs the social events committee, George Custer who runs the parks department, Adolf Hitler runs the holiday planning

113

committee, Marilyn Monroe runs the finance committee, and Mozart who is in charge of the city planning department and, from what is said, does a wonderful job.

"And that concludes our introduction portion. That was a fun six hours, wasn't it? And now, I introduce Eve, she will bring you up to speed on any news items and continue the orientation today."

Walking onto the stage is a beautiful young woman that is dressed in a full business suit and glasses. Her hair is pulled back in a ponytail. She starts with a soft "welcome" then pauses to survey the crowd.

"Today I am here to introduce to you our Patriarch, Satan, and also go over some current events with you. First, let me thank Adam for his wonderful presentation on the leaders of our community and other key personages. Today marks the start of the dance festival over in Liberace Hall. If you are interested, please go to the sign-up table to the left as you exit the building. A reminder to all that next month is March and Jesus's birthday party, so please be courteous and nice to him if you see him around. Next Thursday is Bingo night over at Albert Einstein's garage. OK, now for the moment you have all been waiting for! I introduce to you, Satan himself!"

As she walks off the stage, the ground starts to shake and lights flicker for dramatic effect. Then all the lights go dark and just a spotlight hits the stage, showing a small-statured figure with glasses standing still. He doesn't move as the stunned crowd looks back and forth from the stage to the other people around them and back again. A large smile comes across his face as he clears his throat.

"So, I take it that I am not what you had pictured in your mind?" he chuckles to himself. "Well, I get that a lot. You see, I get confused with my partner, Lucifer, quite often. Plus, you may have noticed that we have a different reputation in the mortal realm than we are in reality. You see, Heaven and Hell are really not that different. There are subtle differences in philosophy but, in general, pretty much the same. We have some folks that are able to pass back and forth as they wish, and there are some, like you guys, that are permanent residents of one or the other. The Mortal Realm is kind of like our chessboard, and the souls are our chess pieces, if you will.

"Allah and I have a friendly wager that has been going on for as long as most of us can remember. Everyone's eternity is brought about by a few key moments in their lives. You may have sensed by now that religion is not a deciding factor at all. Actually, none of the major religions have even more than half of the dogma correct. Basically, we test you and see how you pass the test to decide which side you will go to. Now, there is another place that I have not mentioned that I probably should. The Pit of Despair is the third option. That is a place where the people that have failed miserably in all tests end up.

"There is also a work release program where, before you are escorted to the Pit, you can get a second chance to prove yourself. Everyone gets that opportunity; however, only a precious few make the conversion. The exceptional few that have a very special skill that is needed here, of course, will be enrolled in the program regardless of results. They are, of course, put on a very short leash and watched constantly; we have a few that are running some of our specialty departments that are in that current program. The work release programs are a step above the Pit in that they are still here, but the labors that they must endure are great.

"Let's put that aside for now, shall we? You all must have a lot of questions. Let me try to answer a few of them here.

"First, yes, this is definitely Hell.

"No, you will not be in a torture chamber enduring relentless pain and suffering. Everyone's experience is slightly different and, therefore, what one person has is not the same as what is involved with another person. You are able to interact with each other; I am not sure why people seem to think that when they get here, they can't still be social. If you are sent here from Heaven, I apologize for the repetition you may be experiencing.

"No, I am not Bill Gates. Despite the similarity in appearances, we are not the same person, just distantly related. You all have your itinerary in your domicile, and please, always remember the Rules, as they are the main set of laws here. Other than that, I welcome you all and wish you well."

And with that, the lights all return, and he is gone. We all start to file out of the auditorium and return to our places. I stop to look behind me and take in the sights. It really does look like the regular world that I knew, but slightly different. The mountains in the distance don't seem to have any trees, just like a carpet of green. The sky has light yet no sun. The ground is seemingly made of concrete yet is not as hard. The buildings are all made of some material that I am not aware of. Slowly and leisurely, I wander back to my new home to rest and get ready for my new life.

Day 8

I can't believe it! Not one damn chair in the entire place. No bed. Not even a table I can sit on. There is never any sleep either. Every night is the same thing. I eat a great dinner that is different every night, and then, as I start to unwind from the day's activities, poof. The alarm goes off that the next day is starting. It is a vicious circle and completely diabolical. Everything else is great and a wonderful experience, the people are nice, and there are always activities going on. Yet all I can think about is how I would like to sleep or even just sit down for five minutes.

I saw Jesus the other day but did not get a chance to speak with him. He seems like he is a nice guy; he spends time visiting all of the realms even though he lives in the Heavenly Realm. I notice him and Muhammad are always together. I think they are best friends, at least, looking at it from afar. And that Joan of Arc woman is funny as anything. The other day, she had a group of us in stitches. I hear that she has started spending a lot of time with Guan Yu lately. They seem to be an item. They have started a sports program over near John F. Kennedy's arena. I joined a book club with Confucius and Anastasiya Nikolayevna. We have a great time discussing different writers. Funny turn of events that Confucius has an affinity toward beatnik poetry and Anastasiya loves science fiction novels from the 1950s.

Oh great, it is time for my room inspection, which is pointless, by the way. I never sleep, and there is no bed. Also, the food is automatically cleaned. I think it is just a way of keeping everyone on their toes.

Day 16

Today was a special day. Well, not really. I still have been hunting for a place to sit down, with no luck. I really am getting tired of standing all the time. However, I am getting used to the no-sleep aspect of death. I really barely miss it. But I do long for a chair or something of that nature. I suppose that, too, will be something to get used to as well. The other day, I was introduced to another group of new arrivals. I noticed one really cute woman in the crowd, but I don't know her name. I did catch her glance my way a few times. I was told that there are ways to spend your eternity with more adventurous excursions and activities. I was thinking about signing up for some of the virtual tours with Socrates, but I hear that he gets very technical and loves to add computer graphics to everything.

I have started to forget my previous life and to accept my fate and new existence here. I wonder about the events of my death and how life must have unfolded after I was gone. I think of my family and loved ones and hope that they are all doing well. I start to think if time flows the same here as it does there and if anyone can answer these questions for me. The feeling of longing to know if anyone is thinking of you back in your old life is an odd sensation.

You can get a glimpse of it in the living world, but there is always the possibility of going back to talk to people there. Here, you get this empty sense of wonder, but there is no way to satisfy it, so it becomes a fleeting feeling. I can't understand how someone can feel after hundreds of years of this when you know that so much has changed there.

Day 22

There was an interesting turn of events today. There was a judgment for someone who failed the work release program and was being sent to the Pit of Despair. I have never heard such an agonizing scream before. From the information that I was able to gather, it was for an old dictator that treated his populace in a most cruel fashion. He came here and was given a chance to exist as Satan said everyone gets. However, he never changed or even saw the evil of his ways. He didn't even try to hide his contempt for being here. I could not ascertain the name of the person or their full list of current crimes, but I did gather that he was given the task of janitorial duty at the demon domicile # 13. That is a particularly demanding position since that is where all of the low-level demons reside; those are the ones that have the task of tormenting people in the Mortal Realm that have escaped death in a cruel way. However, I have heard that they have chairs in that building.

I heard that someone was asking about me the other day. I am not sure who it could be, but I am not sure if it would be good to have your name thrown around between others in Hell. Doesn't that kind of seem a bit risky to you? No one can tell me who is doing the asking. I will try to keep a lower profile for a while, just in case.

Day 30

I have completely forgotten the joy of sitting down. The other day, I saw a rock in the park and went to go sit on it, when I got there it turned into a frog. Yes, you heard that right, the large rock turned into a small frog. I almost lost my cool and stepped on the frog, but that would not have been good and would have drawn the attention of the staff.

I have started spending time with someone that I really enjoy. Her name is Camilla, and she is like me in that she arrived a few days after I did. I am not positive, but I believe that I have seen her around here before we officially met. We are still getting used to everything and patterns are starting to form for daily life in our eternity. I am glad to have someone that I trust, but I sometimes wonder why I have trusted her since we first met. I think that she just has that aura around her.

There are some things that we notice and only talk to each other about. I don't want to read too much into it, but I am positive that we are being watched and tested. I also get the feeling that something nefarious is happening here. Imagine that, something nefarious in Hell. Every day there are more people that come, yet there is never any overcrowding. I have noted that every day a few thousand people arrive; however, the streets and dwellings are always roughly the same amount of people.

My room has a slight hum that I have only recently noticed. It is constant and faint. I asked my neighbors and each of them have said that I was crazy and should not mention it to anyone else. Confucius said that I needed to relax and learn to enjoy the little things in death. He has an odd sense of humor that will always make you think and then give a sad sigh as you realize it is basically a bad Dad joke.

Day 37

Camilla has come to meet me every morning for the past week, and we spend pretty much the entire day together until dinner. At that point, I return home and start the evening rituals. She is everything that you could need in a partner for your time in Hell.

She has introduced me to some very intriguing characters. The other day we met up with her friend, who happens to be a demon that works for the president of the Division of Happiness Processing. She is a lovely demon, very pleasant to talk with and is always smiling and laughing. Her horns are a little distracting because they have a large curl that makes them inadvertently point to her breasts. I have become used to living with the demons, so the red skin and horns usually do not even cause a second glance, but for some reason, her uniqueness catches every guy in the room at some point. Her name is Dione, and she is actually related to the daily news woman on the TV. They are cousins but hardly ever see each other. Dione said that her job has many benefits, including being able to spend time with Azazel. She will never admit it, but I believe that she has a sort of crush on him. He is always walking around the middle of the city, and she finds reasons to bump into him.

In her role, she is also able to provide Camilla and me some extra information on the inner workings of Hell that we would not be able to get in other ways. During our lunch, she slipped and told us that they were going to introduce a new head of meditation management. To be honest, I had never even heard of the department until then, but she insisted that it was a huge deal. She explains that some departments are created for the work release programs, like the department that Hitler is assigned to, and others are essential to the functioning of Hell, like the head of meditation management. She tells us that the old department head was found in some place that he should never have been (she wouldn't elaborate on that point but seemed to be very upset at the mention). Needless to say, he was tossed into the Pit without a second thought or trial, so the position was opened. Apparently, Archangel Gabriel himself was going to make an appearance to do the interviews and announcement. It was only the second time I had heard an Archangel's name referenced. They seem to be treated like royalty and a third tier of importance behind only the big guys. Tier one of course is Satan, and tier two consists of Lucifer, Anubis, and Loki. So naturally, I asked about Archangel Gabriel after she mentioned his name. It seemed to me a pretty basic advancement of the conversation. However, Dione's eyes increased about seven times their original size, and her jaw dropped at my mere mentioning of the name.

She then looked around the room and snapped back at me, saying, "You should never speak an Archangel's name, for they can feel when a human being mentions them. I really need to be going now, it was lovely to spend some time with you two," and then was out of the room before we could utter a single response. But it was at this time that I started to notice the hum get louder.

More and more I am curious about the inner workings of this place. But as one would expect, it is very dangerous to ask questions when you are one step away from complete oblivion in the Pit of Despair. I am nervous that, one day, my curiosity will kill the cat, so to speak. Camilla thinks I am overreacting. Maybe I am.

Maybe.

Day 42

Camilla and I have been together every day. I am forever grateful for her comfort and her ever-open ear for me to speak to. We spend days on end walking and talking and moving from place to place. She never wants to stand still in one place, she says that she is nervous that someone will interrupt us in our discussions and break away our concentrations. We talk about our previous lives, and she asks about how I died, but I never reveal too much. I am not sure of the details myself anymore, so I would rather keep the mask of intrigue than admit that I really don't have a clue. I want her to like me for more reasons than that we are just co-inhabitants of Hell. I am sure that she could find much more interesting conversation with just about anyone else. But I find a comfort in the fact that she is here with me now. I wish that we could find a place to sit down and discuss our hopes and dreams without all this motion. I find myself longing for chairs more and more. Did I say chairs? I meant companionship. Or did I? I don't know, maybe I meant both.

I bring her my conspiracy theory about Azazel, and she laughs. She then quickly changes to a grave stare and, in an instant, her beautiful hazel eyes grow serious and almost seem black. "Do not pursue this. You will get yourself into a trouble that you do not understand. Please, for both your sake and mine, drop it."

Instantly, she returns to her normal self and laughs. She always seems to know more than she lets on, but I do not have the capacity to understand women, especially not women in Hell.

Day 59

OK. Maybe I went too far today. I have been poking around just to keep my interest up and keep my mind off of the chair issue. The tree behind the tavern seems to be the key. I am not sure I should say much more at this point. Damn, I wish I had a chair, or at least some ear plugs to drown out that infernal humming.

Day 60

What the hell is wrong with me? I can't seem to stop looking. The tree is definitely the key. I heard it speak to Azazel this afternoon. I could only make out a few words, but it definitely spoke. I think it was talking about a special chair. Or it could have been my mind playing tricks on me. What was that noise? Whew, just the dinner plate refreshing. Azazel is definitely up to something. Dione said that he was talking to Archangel Uriel the other day about an important project. She thought they might be upset about the appointment of a human to the head of meditation management. When the announcement came that Pocahontas was going to get the position, there was a loud murmur amongst the staff. Azazel seemed the most disturbed and has been acting erratically according to Dione. Is that a chair over there? My eyes are just playing tricks on me again. When I saw him wandering around behind the tavern the other day, I decided to start following him. He never seems to pay much attention to the humans around, he kind of views us as the extras in his movie. I have been pretty stealthy in my pursuit on top of that, so I am sure I will be fine.

Camilla insists that I should stop immediately. She thinks I will get caught and will have to sit before Satan to explain myself. Can you believe she said sit before Satan? Recently, I am starting to think that Camilla might not be who she says she is. She says she grew up in Brazil and was traveling to London when she ate something on the plane and choked. That seems a pretty cliché way to die for Hell. I am doubting her story recently, but that is a mystery that must wait for another time. She claims that she is only looking out for me, but we are in Hell, can I really believe her?

Anyway, getting back to what I saw yesterday, it was disturbing to say the least. Azazel started talking to the tree behind the tavern. The first day, I couldn't make out anything, but today I was closer. Can you believe the tree talked back to him? It honest to God talked to him. Oddly, I think it has a Canadian accent; it might be a maple tree. I think tomorrow I will be waiting early at the tree to try to catch the conversation completely. The alarm is about to go off to start the new day.

Day 65

I can't believe that they were talking about the chairman position on a council of demons. It, unfortunately, had nothing to do with a physical chair. And to think I risked so much just getting involved in demon politics. After all that, they had a revolt and Satan allowed an emergency election to replace the chairman of the governing committee. Azazel was elected to that position, and he has already made a petition to Satan regarding an advisory position above the head of meditation management. It seems that this position is very important to the demon staff. They all insist that a demon should be the head. Politics are the same, it seems, whether it be human or demon politics.

Camilla tells me that she thinks I was noticed following Azazel the other day. She is worried that my movements are most likely being watched carefully now. I still don't know if I can trust her, but she may have a good point. There was a new person in the book club yesterday, he just introduced himself as "Tim." Tim ended up standing right behind me the whole time. He even said his favorite writer was Mark Twain. If that isn't suspicious, then I don't know what is. That's like someone saying their favorite book is Moby Dick. If that is your answer, then you are hiding something.

I think that I threw him off a little today though. He asked me if I had any recommendations for other clubs he could join. So I told him that there was a club that met in the tavern every week called the drinking club.

"They show up and drink for the day, and they usually don't speak to each other. I don't even think that they have a sign-in sheet. You just bring money and drink the day away. You should try it."

By the time he realizes there is no club, that it is just drunkards that haven't moved past their addictions from the living world, I will have readjusted my schedule and figured out the Camilla conundrum. Tim. Couldn't they come up with a better spy name than Tim?

Day 66

Camilla and Dione are always together now, I don't even remember when they weren't side by side. Camilla said it is because they understand each other, but I often wonder if it isn't something more. Today, on the way back from our daily excursions, they were whispering something while walking behind me. Then they started to giggle like little schoolgirls. I turned around, and they both started looking away and laughing. I felt like I was the butt of a joke that I wasn't privy to. Camilla said she wanted to spend time together tomorrow, just the two of us. Dione then started singing like Grover Washington Jr., "Just the two of us...we can make it if we try."

Maybe tomorrow I will ask her what it is about.

Day 67

Camilla, today, spent the whole day with me and was very sweet. It was a wonderful day and everything seemed so lighthearted compared to the recent events. Maybe it is just my mind finally getting through the conspiracy theories. I have started to think that I have been getting all worked up over nothing, and I feel regret over being suspicious of Camilla. I asked her about the day before, and she just said that it doesn't matter, that she had something to ask me later. We walked around the whole city; it was as if we were two school kids in love. We held hands and talked softly about little things we loved about the Mortal Realm and even here in Hell. She even suggested for us to go to the sauna together. She said she had a reservation for us. Once there, we were escorted into the room and asked to undress. When we started to relax, she started the conversation.

"Do you ever think about the future here? I mean, really think about it?" she asked while we stood naked in the sauna together.

It felt like we were alone even though there were about 30 other people in there with us. For the first time, in a long time, my mind was swimming with thoughts other than conspiracy theories or chairs. I was feeling dizzy and intoxicated by her voice. I wasn't even concerned about my nudity or distracted by hers. I just felt the cliché warm and fuzzy. I looked into her eyes and found a relief that I hadn't realized that I had missed. It was at this moment that I noticed the red glare in her eyes. It was faint, but definitely there. It didn't fully register at the time but did fold back into the recesses of my mind for reflection later. She continued to speak as though we were the only two people in existence.

"Well? I have been recently, and I wanted to see what you thought. There is so much that we have seen and experienced since you arrived here. I feel so comfortable with you. Do you know that there have been stories of demons and humans becoming pairs and living through eternity together? Kind of like a real Romeo and Juliet story. Did you know that Pocahontas is paired with an Archangel? There are rumors that she got one of the most important positions in Hell just because of that connection. I do not believe that is the only reason however.

"I am sorry, enough about other women, today is about you and me. Do you ever think of me when we are apart? I think of you constantly. Dione thinks that I am obsessed. I denied it for the longest time but have recently started to ponder its validity. When I am near you, both of my hearts pound faster than normal. My skin almost feels like it is burning red again. I want to tell you everything even though it will cost me dearly. You have become my meaningful existence. I want to tell my father, but I am afraid he would never approve. I mean, can you imagine Satan's daughter falling in love with a human?

"I wonder how you will react when the sauna enchantment ends and you can respond again. The control of your mind is only temporary, please do not be afraid or angry with me. I only wanted to tell you my feelings and my wishes, and this was the best way that I could think of. I know that there will be difficulties and hardships that you and I will need to endure. But if you could only feel the same for me, we can persevere and our love can last an eternity or two.

"One last minute to try to explain. Why does time go so fast when we do not wish it to? Let me start by saying, I was assigned to you at first, as you were identified as a person of interest to the council. I do not know the details, nor do I really care, but something about the way you died had raised a concern with you being here. As I spent time with you, I realized two troublesome facts. One was that I was falling in love with you more and more every day. You! A human of all things! I had never felt these emotions before, not only did I care about your well-being, but I increasingly wanted to become a bigger part of your life. And the second fact was also clear...you don't belong here. No matter how much I want you to."

I awake from the hazy feeling and was again in the sauna with Camilla. I shake my head to get some clarity back to my mind. She was just staring at me with tears welling up in her eyes. At that moment, I realized that it wasn't a daydream, it was real. The whole time we had been in a moment together, and she was pouring her soul out to me. It was also at that time that I started to notice her skin was slowly darkening and becoming a shade of red that rivaled Dione's. Her eyes shifted from the hazel that I had shared laughs and concerns with to become a darker shade of black than I have ever experienced. However, I was not frightened at all. For some reason, it was the exact opposite.

A deep and sinister smile came through my lips as I stared back at her concerned face. Her concern turned to a puzzled expression as I started to laugh a full deep and hardy laugh. I started to feel the tears running down my face and my mind instantly clear, like the winter sky after a harsh snowstorm leaves the landscape cold, still, and brisk. In an instant, I stopped laughing and gave her a cold dark stare. The silence between us was for dramatic effect, and I was calculating my response in the most sinister manner: that of a lover who understands they control all of the power in the relationship. I felt her expression change from puzzled astonishment to the same realization of defeat that I knew I was exuding. My devious smile broke into a soft, loving expression. Gingerly, I whispered, "My love, somehow, I always knew, but could never imagine how you felt. I tell you now that I will be yours and will love you beyond the extent of mere mortals or immortals. I will bring you to the precious precipice of emotions of which you have never experienced in all eternity. I only have one thing to ask. Can you bring me a chair to sit on?"

One Hour and Fifteen Minutes

Chapter 1

There she is. I gave everything I had for one hour and fifteen minutes with her. Can you blame me? Look at her incredible legs. Her body is breathtaking. Her breasts are perfect; not big but not small, just perfect. She is in great shape, well-toned but not muscle-bound. Her sparkling blue eyes shine into your soul. Her long blonde hair is beautifully draped over her shoulders. Her smile haunts me every time I close my eyes. She is smart, funny, and well-spoken. As if all of that wasn't enough to make you cry out her name in agony, she is rich and famous as well. I can boldly say that we were in love for exactly one hour and fifteen minutes.

How, you ask? Why would such a woman even glance in my direction, let alone love someone like me? That is a story that I will gladly tell because, even though it doesn't have a happy ending, at least not for me, I have nothing but time to tell it. But before I get into that, let me introduce myself. I am Calvin Theodore Jackson. My friends call me CT, but I am nobody special, just another face in the crowd. When I met her, I was 19 years old and living in New York City. I had a small place that I could barely afford and not a cent to my name in the bank. She was 20 and acting in major motion pictures. From the first time I saw her, I knew she was my heart's desire. She, of course, had no idea who I was, nor did she even know that I existed. In the end, I guess I always knew it would never last, even if it did happen. I mean, look at her, what could I offer her that would make her happier than she already was. It was always hopeless, but in the end, for one hour and fifteen minutes, I was the love of her life.

Her name is Jennifer Vernon. She was born in the suburbs of Philadelphia. Her mother was a fifth-grade teacher, and her father was a lawyer. She is an only child and started acting at the age of 17. She got her first break in the summer blockbuster, *A Hard Place*. She stole the show and was nominated for an Oscar that year. Not a bad way to start a career, and she continued starring in hit movies for the next three years. Veteran movie stars all wanted her to co-star in their next film, and her career was officially a high-profile success. It was at this point that I met her.

At the time, I had a job at a music store in the Village. Not really a big place, but a good store that was well known. She walked in one day, and immediately, her beauty enamored me. She was just walking around the store looking through CDs, without the entourage of people around her like many other stars always had. It seemed as if time had slowed down, like in all of those stupid romance movies. She had captivated my attention so blindly that I fell down the stairs and landed right next to her. As I laid face down in the carpet, I heard an angelic giggle and looked up at her. She laughed again and offered out her hand to help me up. I could barely think but took her hand and stood up.

"Thanks, I must have missed that first step. Excuse me, but aren't you Jennifer Vernon?"

She gave a sexy smile as she said, "Yeah, and you must be CT."

I was mystified. How did *she* know my name? Was this destiny?

"Uh, how do you know my name?" I asked with unparalleled grace.

"Well, I am a pretty adept reader and read your nametag. Are you OK? That was a pretty good drop, I have seen stuntmen get hurt on lesser falls."

"Yeah, I am fine. It happens sometimes, I guess. Are you OK?" What kind of stupid question was that? Let's rewind this a few seconds and take a slower look. An incredibly beautiful woman giggles and helps me up asking if I am OK, and my reply was this: "Yeah, I am fine. It happens sometimes, I guess. Are you OK?" It really was a wonder that I had ever had a girlfriend at all, ever. Now, you may be surprised when I tell you that I have never really been a Don Juan, but I had had a few girlfriends in my life. OK, so only two. But that doesn't excuse the eloquent dialog between this amazing woman and me. Now, where was I? Oh yeah, Don Juan said, "Are you OK?"

"Umm, OK, maybe you hurt your head more than you think, you were the one that fell remember? Oh well, anyway, do you have any new release CDs?"

Ouch, the subject changed to business. "Oh, yeah, we have them over here." I escorted her to the CD rack and limped away, never taking my eyes off of her. I was smitten. Whispering to myself, I mumbled, "I would give anything for her and I to be in love, if even for just an hour and fifteen minutes. Man, she is incredible." Soon after she left the store that day, my story truly began.

Moments after she walked out of the door, a small frail old man walked in. Now, at the time, I didn't really understand what was about to transpire, but looking back, it really should have set off a few alarm bells in my head. The man walked right up to me and started what seemed like a sales pitch.

"Hello, young man! She really is a beautiful woman, isn't she?"

At that, I shook my head in agreement, still staring out the window. I turned to get an overview of this little man, looking him up and down. He really wasn't as old as your first glance would have led you to believe, but had an elderly demeanor, almost as if he was taken right out of the 1940s. He kind of had the look of George Burns meets Humphrey Bogart. Well, maybe it was just the old hat and the cigar that gave him that look. His suit was old as well and looked like it was bought in 1920 and left in a closet until 1980 but then worn every day since. His marble-like black eyes sparkled and gave him a sinister look. He took off his hat and held it loosely in his hands by the rim. As he talked, he slowly turned the hat counter clockwise in his hands.

"Well, my son, today is just your lucky day, isn't it? What I have for you is a once in a lifetime deal."

"That's OK, sir. I am not interested in buying any toasters or vacuums or whatever."

"Ah, but you misunderstand me. What I offer is more than you ever could dream of. I offer wealth, power, fame, and...love. Would you really give anything to be with that woman? If so, I can make it happen."

As he said this, he tilted his head slightly and looked me up and down. It was almost as if he was looking through me.

"Who are you? Is this some kind of a prank or something? Oh, I get it. This is one of those joke TV shows where Jaime Kennedy or Ashton Kutcher is going to jump out and show the hidden camera is inside your hat or something."

"No, I am afraid it is not a joke. What I offer is far beyond your comprehension, but let's just say it is an even swap, so to speak."

"How would you possibly be able to get that girl to be interested in me?"

"Let's just say that I know her personally and would be able to arrange something for you. Are you interested?"

Now, I know what you are thinking. Is this guy really that stupid? Well, I guess I am, or at least, I was. It never even dawned on me that this might be a bad situation to get into.

"Maybe, what are we talking about here?" I questioned him skeptically.

"CT, may I call you Calvin? I find that it is more comforting using first names rather than nicknames."

"Sure, whatever you want, sir, and what is your name?"

"My name is Stan Adams Putii, but you may call me Stan, if you'd like."

At that point, he had a strangely deviant smirk on his face, which should have tipped me off to his mischievous nature. It didn't, but it should have.

"Great, now all that I ask is that you are honest with me. It will make everything work out better if you are honest. Not only honest to me, but also to yourself. How can you make your life perfect for yourself if you don't admit what you really want?"

Chapter 2

Stan Adams Putii…

If I were a smarter man, I would have gotten the joke. It really is clever if you think about it. Alas, I let the whole situation continue when I should have walked away before it got any worse for me.

"What do you mean make my whole life perfect?"

"You do want to be with that woman, don't you? What was it you said, if even for an hour and fifteen minutes? The difference in the grand scheme of things matters little to me, but this I can make happen for you."

Again, knowing then what I know now would have helped greatly, since, at the time, I still didn't get it. The next sentence out of my mouth might never have been uttered.

"Yeah, of course I would give anything to have her be in love with me, but that doesn't mean it can happen."

"If you sign this contract, I can make it happen."

As he slid the paper out of his inside shirt pocket (seemingly shooting sparks against his suit, which caused me to rub my eyes in disbelief), I saw her standing across the street. Her beauty seemed to be glowing and almost taunting me. I looked back at the old man, and he had a fiendish look on his face.

"You still don't understand what I am offering you, do you? You really aren't too quick under the top hat, are you? Have you thought much about your place in the universe? Your purpose? Your true purpose?"

As he said those words, he leaned in closer toward me, and as I looked in his marble-like eyes, I saw a scene I could not possibly describe. Just then, everything became clear. He wasn't talking about any kind of new gadget or life insurance; it was actually a new life he was offering. At once, I became both frightened and further intrigued at the same time. It is a defining moment in one's life when everything in the universe starts to reveal itself.

It's a farce; the whole universe is a damn grand hoax. It is just one big game played by two sick deities. In one instant, the faux universe revealed itself to a lonely retail clerk in a music store. I guess, in a way, I kind of always felt the twisted game being played around me, but it still is a rattling revelation. To tell you the truth, I wish I never had found out. Kind of like when I was told that there wasn't really a Santa Claus; I was so disenchanted that Christmas lost all joy. The empty pit in my stomach swallowed me whole. Yet nothing could prepare me for what was to come next.

"Now you see, don't you? I can give you what you desire. I can give you what is deepest in your heart." He seemed to lure me in magically, no, almost hypnotically.

But how could this be? I had always believed in my faith and tried to live a good life, but this was too much. To come this close to understanding it, only to find out that everything is not what it seems. Mankind has been set up as the greatest rouse of all time. My mind was reeling from too much information. As I tried to get a grip on my thoughts, the old man began to shake his head as if he was losing his patience. Perplexed, I questioned his motives.

"So, what do I give you for this 'perfect' life? Do I have to give you my soul?"

"Not give, just pledge its loyalty to me. The soul is not what you think it is. As I have just shown you, things are not exactly as your religions have explained it to you. The universe is a form of...soul control, if you will. But the soul still has full free will and can control its own destiny until it has pledged an allegiance, until it is needed, which will complete its journey. There is not as much difference in the two deities as your faiths have suggested. In 'reality,' we are actually friends, but this little experimental existence you enjoy has provoked quite a bit of friendly competition between us.

"Since we are speaking freely, plus the fact that I can erase every aspect of this encounter from your memory, I will divulge some privileged information to you. My counterpart's name is Tom Gladighy. He is more a hands-off type of a manager than myself. He only gets involved in larger scaled events such as wars, plagues, and natural disasters for example. Whereas I believe every smaller encounter can generate more success. It is not a matter of good or evil or wrong or right. These are concepts that mankind has placed on itself. Although I find them quite fascinating, I rarely see the true difference between them. It all comes down to your perspective in the situation; what one person finds evil, another finds just. Take the Cold War between the US and USSR. Each side believed, with all of their being, that the other was the evil empire, when, in reality, they were both the same, just governments with different ways of controlling the populace."

"I find this is quite apparent, yet all of your wars and confrontations are a product of mankind's lack of sense to see this. If you stand back and watch it unfold, it is actually kind of humorous. Not necessarily the millions of deaths involved but the situations that caused them. Your World War II, for example, was caused because one man blamed an entire religion for an unfortunate incident he had. Adolf Hitler was upset because a Jewish man refused to refund his money at a deli for a sandwich that made him ill. Since this was shortly after he had been called a failure in the art world, also run by Jewish aristocracy, he snapped. Then he began to blame the Jews for everything that was wrong with the world. Well, wrong in his eyes, that is. It snowballed from there. But if he would have stepped back and noticed that he was the one that had left the sandwich out in the sun for an hour before he ate it, then he would have seen that he was to blame for the food going bad. If he also had requested that he wanted to be a good artist and specified what he wanted to be famous for, it would have greatly helped him remain mentally stable, but he just asked to be an artist and to be famous. Hence, World War II would never have happened if he paid attention to details."

"What do you mean requested? Did you have a deal with Hitler?" I blurted out in shock.

"Have you had your Ritalin today? Hitler is not the point, my dear boy, please stay focused on the task at hand. The point is that what one person views as just, another sees as unjust. What one determines as evil, another judges divine. That is the nature of the human species; you view everything through the individual's eyes and not through humanities eyes. Like I stated before, your being involved with this girl makes no difference to the world, but would it not make you happy? Why not be happy and enjoy life instead of just coasting by in it?"

"Yes, I would very much like to be with her. There are still many questions I have though."

"Questions, questions, questions. Can you not see this opportunity? Do you not wish to have a 'perfect' life? If you are uninterested, I will leave."

"No! Wait, don't leave, I apologize," I stated with panic in my voice. I did not want to let this opportunity get away without even giving it a shot.

"Good, now let's get down to business." He shook out the piece of paper he produced from his pocket earlier and placed it on the counter. Pulling out an odd-looking pen, he stated, "Now, this contract is binding for the length of your soul and, in being as such, must be signed in your own blood. The pen I have here uses no ink, it writes in blood, your blood. Please sign here."

In pricking my finger once with the pen, there was enough to sign my entire name (in triplicate, of course). Immediately after completing the signature, the contract disappeared in a puff of smoke. Returning the old hat to his head, he gave a diabolical laugh and said, "So it is done."

As he turned to leave, he nodded his head out the window, never taking his eyes off of my bewildered face. When my gaze left his face and looked outside, I gasped aloud. She was coming back!

"Your time starts when she walks through that door. Now I bid you farewell…for now at least." He turned and opened the door for her to walk in as he left.

Chapter 3

Just then it hit me. Time? How much time? Should I have read the contract? What did I just do? But all of that faded instantly when she walked right up and kissed me. I was immediately lost in her eyes. Those deep blue eyes almost completely immobilized me in a moment. I looked outside and the old man was nowhere in sight. We left together right away and got into her car. After she told the driver to take her to the hotel, neither of us said another word. Me because I was dumbfounded, and her because she seemed to be completely lost in thought, almost sleepwalking.

Her driver took us to her hotel. He was a chubby little man with a smooth round face. He seemed very pleasant, but then again, that was part of his job. Once at the hotel, we walked right in and took the elevator to her room. Her room, which was bigger than both of my first two apartments combined, had two giant rooms, a living room and a bedroom. When we walked through the door, the clock rang twelve o'clock. It had been eleven forty-five when she walked in the store the second time. As I looked at the clock, I thought I saw the shadow of Stan Adams Putii staring back at me with that same devious smile on his face. Then it hit me. Could I have been that stupid? Did I really sell my soul for only an hour and fifteen minutes? That would mean I only had an hour left. What would happen then? Would I just disappear? Would I die right then and there? What would I do in that next hour? I know what my original thought was for the hour, but is it ethical to do that knowing that she might actually be manipulated into it against her own free will? Or was she? Did she really like me and this was just a push in that direction?

As I was pondering all of this, she grabbed my collar dragged me into the bedroom. After she threw me on the bed, I lost all inhibitions and reservations and drowned myself in her beauty. Three and a half minutes later, I was sweaty and lying next to the girl of my dreams. All I wanted to do was explain myself and pray that she understood my plight. With a half-smile, she stared in my eyes as if she already knew. Kissing her, I grabbed her and pulled her on top of me. Hey, I did have a time limit, didn't I?

Five minutes after that, I sat on the edge of her giant hotel bed. Looking at the clock, which now read 12:10, I wondered how many others had been swindled by Mr. Putii. Which then led me to Tom Gladighy. Who was he? Did he know what was going on? Two soft hands ran over my back and shoulders, and it brought me back to this moment. Deciding to seize the moment, I turned and asked her to tell me about herself. I wanted to know every intimate detail. If this was my final hour, well forty-seven and a half minutes now, I wanted to really know the person I gave everything for. She told me about her childhood, career, and parents. I asked stupid questions like, "How is it being really famous? Do you like all the attention?"

Now it was 12:30. She asked if I wanted to go out to get something to eat. I declined and said I just wanted to have her to myself for a while. Not untrue, of course, but really, how could I waste any more time with travel. So she ordered from room service. Wrapping herself in a robe, she got out of bed and walked into the other room. Never in my life have I ever been so aware of time, which I found actually does move slower when you pay attention to it (in this case, that was a good thing).

Putting a robe on myself, I joined her in the other room. She was getting a bottle of water from the small refrigerator. It was then that I noticed that she also was watching the clock. Was there someplace she was supposed to be that I was keeping her from? Did she know that I was on a time limit? Maybe she worked for Mr. Putii and was in on the scam. I didn't really believe that, but I was grasping at anything at that point. Noticing that I had entered the room, she turned and walked toward me. It was then I perceived the small sadness in her smile. It was as if she were hiding her despair. When she got closer, I took her in my arms and held her. I wanted to comfort her. I wanted to make her happy. She was all I had left, and I wanted to be remembered by her in a positive way. I asked her if there was anything I could do for her to make her happy. With a slight whimper, all she said was, "Please don't leave me."

At that, I picked her up and carried her back to bed. We just held each other for the remaining 25 minutes, barely saying a word. At 12:59, there was a knock at the door.

"Room Service, Ms. Vernon," came a raspy familiar voice.

We both got up and went to the door. Almost on cue with the door opening, the clock struck one.

"Or should I say, my two wonderful new acquisitions?"

Chapter 4

It wasn't the shock of seeing Stan Adams Putii that caught me off guard, but the way he was dressed and what he said. He was the same old man that had come into the store, but different. He had on a brand new suit (it almost looked like a tuxedo). He was without his hat but did, still, have the cigar in his hand. It was as if time had stopped. There wasn't a noise anywhere. The slight hum of the traffic outside was gone, even the clock stopped ticking. When he walked inside, it dawned on me that he had said "two new acquisitions." I was overcome with horror. Did I sign away her life as well? I couldn't have, could I? My horror slightly dissipated as I realized that Jennifer obviously knew Mr. Putii as well. She seemed to cower in his presence, as if she also knew his origin and was expecting his visit.

"How do you know her?" I asked softly. She twisted in quick realization that I knew him as well as she knew him, in that same sad and devilish way. Stan Adams Putii closed the door behind him without touching it and sat in the large chair in the middle of the room. He began to describe his infernal tale to us.

"Did either of you really believe that you were my only clients? How naive. You surprise me the most, Ms. Vernon.

I have always liked the savvy, intelligent way you present yourself, and always, I thought you were quite bright. On the other hand, we have our new friend here, Mr. Jackson. Calvin here is what we might call intellectually challenged when it comes to matters like these, or any matter actually. I would expect him to be confused, but you, my dear? How disappointing."

Sitting there in that chair, he looked even more fiendish than before. His smile now seemed half crooked, and he started to light his cigar. "How well things always time out. It was with only a slight manipulation that Calvin asked for his contract on the exact day that your contract had expired. I was very pleased at that development. You see, contrary to common belief, I do not monitor everyone everywhere for deals. I only choose the right people at the right time. Calvin, is everything alright? You still look quite perplexed, my boy."

Then came the line that made everything clear to me at that time. The line that I had thought earlier but did not dare want to utter.

Stan Adams Putii confirmed: "I am Satan, stupid!"

I fumbled the question I already knew the answer to: "And that means the man you mentioned earlier, Tom Gladighy is, is…" my voice faded.

"Ah, yes, he is God Almighty himself," he said with a puff of cigar smoke that seemed to fill the room thickly, cutting off the oxygen supply.

I turned and looked at Jennifer who was nodding her head in silent agreement. Her gaze was dejectedly fixed on our friend in the chair.

"You see, I met Jennifer three and a half years ago. She was just this simple girl from Philly who was dreaming of being an actress, but she really didn't have the talent or the drive to make it happen on her own. Did you, my dear?"

Lowering her head, Jennifer murmured, "Yeah."

With a swift move of his hand, he reproduced two documents from his inside suit pocket. Placing them forcefully on the table next to him, he looked at us wantonly.

"Now, are you both ready to conclude our arrangements? I may be able to halt time, but really, I should get to my other clients." As he stated this, he looked at a rather old-looking watch around his wrist.

Jennifer then, with a pang of shock, turned to me and asked, "Wait a minute, so what was your contract for? Did you just sell your soul to have sex with me? What kind of a creep loser are you?"

Feeling the need to plead for her forgiveness, I stuttered, "No. I mean, not exactly. It was more like I wanted to have you be in love with me. It was my neglect for details that let us only have an hour and fifteen minutes together. Which I still contend was a deliberate trick He hid from me."

Looking at me with a sort of disgusted pity, she dropped to her knees and whimpered, "Please, God, help us! What have I done? I don't want to go to Hell!"

"Now, Now. There will be no need for tears or pleading cries to God for help. Unlike what you see in the movies, we do not interfere with each other's projects. It is against the rules of our little wager. Stand up, my dear." Mr. Putii stood up quickly and grabbed Jennifer's arm. "It is all in good taste. It really isn't as bad as your religious folks have made it out to be. There is no fire or burning flesh or anything like that. Actually, I find the temperature quite pleasant. The food is rather bad, if you bother to eat, which is why I eat down here more often than not. But what people tell me is that you get used to it." He smiled his evil smile and again looked at his watch. "We really must be going."

Before I realized I said it, I exclaimed, "Why do you keep looking at your watch? I would expect the all-powerful Devil not to be on a deadline." After it slipped out, I realized that I might have just offended Satan, and nothing good can come of that.

But he just calmly grinned and explained, "You see, as I stated earlier, I can halt time, not stop it completely forever. This watch, as you have called it, is actually telling me how much time there is before time returns to normal. Kind of like an oven timer. It beeps when the turkeys are cooked. Are you ready now, my turkeys?" At that, I thought I heard a faint giggle from Jennifer. Turning to look at her, I noticed that she had the look of someone who had just realized her fate and accepted it with a giddy fear. I wish that I had taken her cue instead of evoking more annoyance from the man that was Stan Adams Putii.

Of course, I could not just let everything flow down its inevitable path; I provoked him by stating, "This sucks! Is there no way for an appeal or any way to contact God to explain our case? Is everything your final word? I can't believe that. I mean, you aren't even all powerful or even very frightening!"

And at that, I heard Jennifer scream, "What are you saying, you ass!"

A dark foreboding look crossed Satan's face, and his person became distorted and smoky. The room started to shake and grew darker by the second. Stan Adams Putii became…something else. It wasn't as novel as the creatures that you see on TV and in the movies. This was actually terrifying. It didn't have horns, red skin, or any other cliché markings. This was just pure evil. For a split second, all I could I hear was an echoed voice, "You have no notion of what evil is! You can come quietly and nicely, or you can insist on the alternative. This is your last chance, Calvin Theodore Jackson!"

The voice was so painfully loud that my eyes started to tear up (at least that is what I tell people). With the tears running down my face, I cried, "I am sorry. I will go quietly! Please!"

Instantly, the room returned to normal with a few minor changes. There was lightly splattered blood on the wall in front of us. On the table, where the contracts were, there was another piece of paper. It was blank. That is, blank until, in my own handwriting, a note appeared. It read:

Dear world,

I could not stand by and watch this perfect angel be soiled by fame and riches. She is the perfection of the female ideal, and since she would not let me protect and love her, I had no other choice. Her body and legacy are now forever safe. If I could not have her to myself, no one would spoil her innocence.

We shall be together in the next world!

C.T.

My jaw dropped to the floor, and I looked at the bed in the other room. Following my gaze, Jennifer screamed as the scene unfolded before us. First, the blood seeped into the disheveled sheets, then they slowly became raised, as if they contained a quiet sleeping body. Spots of splattered blood dripped down the wall in tiny rivers of red. As we followed the progression of events unfolding before us, two hands fell softly on our shoulders. It was the sinister form of Stan Adams Putii standing behind us, glowing of villainous pride. I returned my focus to the scene and noticed a body on the floor next to the bed. All I needed to see were the feet to know that it was my body lying there. In the bed, Jennifer's perfect body lay peacefully still.

I held Jennifer's hand as I somberly asked, "So this is how it will be wrapped up. It is rather clean. I do have to give you credit for that. So what happens next?" Jennifer noticed my hand in hers and pulled away in horror. In that exact second, time started to flow forward again. This time, it was surprisingly going faster. With the room spinning in a blur, everything faded, and all I could see was the smile on Stan Adams Putii's demonic face. The next thing I remember is waking up here. That is my tale, my curse. I have been here for god who knows how long, and all I can do is wait. This one small blank room is all I have seen in an unbearable amount of time. I have no one around; there is no sense of, well, anything actually. I sit in my stiff uncomfortable plastic chair and wait. Too terrified by what I might find, I never get up and walk around. Every now and then, I ask myself the same questions. Is this really Hell? If so, it is worse than I could have suspected. The unrelenting waiting for something to happen is unexplainably the worst torture there could be. What would my life have been like if I had declined that diabolical offer? Would I have led a worthy and beneficial life? What happened to Jennifer Vernon? Was she suffering the same fate, or did she have a different personal Hell? The most pressing question, that returns almost on cue, is the most perplexing to answer. Was it all worth it? Was that hour and fifteen minutes worth an eternity of this? Well, it really was an amazing hour and fifteen minutes.